CAPE MAY BEACH BUMS

CLAUDIA VANCE

CHAPTER ONE

The morning crowd at Ostara's Coffee House was already in full swing. Liz joined the line, the espresso machine hissing behind the counter, the smell of fresh coffee and pastries in the air.

Furnish & Feast had only been open for about a month, and while the business was thriving beyond their expectations, the learning curve had been steep. Between managing her furniture restoration workshop and helping Greg keep the whole operation running smoothly, she'd barely had time to catch her breath. Today, Greg had insisted she take the morning off, promising that Patrick could handle any customers on her side of the shop.

"You need a break," he'd said that morning. "Go take a walk. Remember what it's like to be a customer somewhere."

So here she was, waiting in line like a normal person, scrolling through her phone and only half paying attention to the murmur of conversations around her.

"Liz? Is that you?"

She looked up from her phone, momentarily confused. A woman about her age stood a few people ahead in line, waving enthusiastically with both hands. Her dark hair was piled on top of her head in a haphazard bun held together with what looked like two paintbrushes, and she wore an oversized kimono jacket covered in abstract swirls of orange and teal over a long flowy shirt and baggy patchwork jeans. A collection of chunky beaded necklaces clattered against each other as she bounced on her heels.

"It's Megan. Megan Hudson. From Moore College of Art? Oh my gosh, this is wild. This is absolutely wild."

The name clicked into place, and Liz couldn't help but laugh. "Megan! Wow, it's been years."

Megan stepped out of line and pulled Liz into a hug. "Twenty years at least. Maybe more? I can't believe you're here. Do you live in Cape May now?"

"I do," Liz said, still processing the surprise of seeing her old classmate. "My husband and I moved back years ago. We actually just opened a café and furniture restoration place called Furnish and Feast."

Megan's eyes widened. "Wait, wait, wait. That gorgeous place with the big windows? The one with all the—" She made a vague gesture with her hands. "The vibe? I walked by it the other day and almost went in, but I was running late for a meeting. Or maybe it was the day before? I remember thinking, whoever designed that space really gets it."

"That's us," Liz said, feeling proud.

"I saw something online about it. Some vlogger? Or maybe it was Instagram. One of those things." Megan shrugged. "But it looked amazing. I always knew you'd do something great with design. You were the most talented person in our program. Like, by far. Everyone thought so."

Liz felt herself blush. "That's generous of you. But what about you? Last I heard, you were headed to New York to work for that gallery."

Something in Megan's expression shifted before she composed herself. "Oh, you know, I did the gallery thing for a while, then moved into—what do they call it—arts administration? Event coordination, installation design, that whole world. It's very—" She circled her hand in the air as if trying to conjure the right word. "Anyway, that's why I'm in Cape May."

The line moved forward, and they shuffled along with it.

"I'm working on the Luminous Festival," Megan said, her voice picking up speed. "The light art installation? It's opening tonight. Tonight! And I'm the lead coordinator for the whole Cape May installation, which is exciting, obviously, but also completely terrifying."

The banners were everywhere around town—the festival would transform the beach and various locations into an outdoor gallery of light-based art.

"That's incredible," Liz said. "I've heard it's supposed to be spectacular."

Megan let out a laugh that sounded more exhausted than amused. "It's supposed to be. If we can pull it off." She reached the counter and ordered a large cold brew with an extra shot, then waited while Liz ordered her cappuccino.

Once they had their drinks, Megan gestured toward an empty table near the window. "Do you have a few minutes? I would love to catch up."

"Sure," Liz said.

They settled into chairs across from each other, and Liz noticed the dark circles under Megan's eyes that her makeup couldn't quite conceal. She looked frazzled in a way that went beyond normal event-planning stress.

"So tell me everything," Liz said. "How did you end up coordinating a major light festival?"

Megan took a long sip of her coffee before answering. "So I've been with Luminous for, like, three years? We do these traveling installations all over the world—Paris, Tokyo, Sydney —and when they said Cape May, I practically begged for it. I mean, remember how we used to come down here on week-ends during school? A beach town! Historic architecture! The energy here is just—" She kissed her fingertips like a chef. "I thought it would be perfect. But then." She let out a long breath. "Then reality happened."

"What happened?" Liz asked.

Megan set her cup down and started ticking things off on her fingers. "My assistant coordinator quit. Just—poof—gone. Two weeks ago. No notice, no nothing. And one of our artists, the one doing the kinetic piece, family emergency, can't be here. And the light installation on the beach? The interactive one? It keeps—" She made a sputtering sound with her lips. "Salt air and electronics, apparently. Who knew? I mean, someone should have known. And I have forty vendors and volunteers who keep asking me questions I don't have answers to, and I'm just one person, Liz. One person with two paintbrushes holding her hair up and a very expensive caffeine habit."

Liz listened, recognizing the familiar signs of someone drowning in responsibilities.

"But the worst part," Megan continued, leaning forward, "is that it doesn't feel right. The whole thing. It's like—" She paused. "The energy isn't flowing. The pieces are all there, but they're not talking to each other, you know? There's no—" She made a swooping gesture. "No journey. And that was always my thing, right? In school? I could make things happen, but the big-picture vision stuff?" She pointed at Liz. "That was you. That was always you."

Liz remembered. Their senior project had been a collaborative effort, with Megan handling logistics and execution while Liz designed the overall concept. They'd made a good team.

"What about the organization?" Liz asked. "Can't they send someone to help?"

"Ha!" The laugh came out a little too loud. "Everyone's stretched thin. We have like three other installations happening right now. Berlin, I think? And somewhere in Australia?" She shook her head. "The point is, I'm on my own here, and if this tanks, it's my name. My reputation. Everything." She looked down at her coffee. "I'm honestly kind of freaking out, Liz."

Liz winced. She knew what it was like to pour yourself into something and fear it might not be enough.

"What would help most right now?" Liz asked.

Megan looked at her, and there was desperation in her eyes. "Someone with an actual eye for design. Someone who can walk through everything with me and tell me what's off, because I know something's off, I can feel it, but I can't see it anymore. I've been staring at it too long." Her voice dropped. "You always had that gift, Liz. You could look at a space and just know."

Before Liz could respond, Megan kept going.

"I'm not asking you to, like, take over or anything. Just a few hours. Today. Walk through it with me, tell me what you see, and I'll pay you. Obviously. Whatever your rate is. I don't even know what your rate is, but whatever it is, it's fine. This is —" She pressed her hands together like she was praying. "I really need this, Liz."

It was her day off. Greg had practically pushed her out the door. And when was the last time she'd done pure design work? Not since she'd closed her interior design business.

"Okay," Liz said. "I'll help."

The relief on Megan's face was immediate. "Oh, thank goodness. Thank you. Seriously. You have no idea." She clutched her chest. "I was literally just standing in line thinking about how everything is falling apart, and then there you were. It's like the universe sent you."

"Don't thank me yet," Liz said. "You haven't seen my rates."

Megan laughed. "Whatever it is, worth it. Totally worth it." She was already grabbing her bag and standing up. "Can we go now? I know that's pushy. I'm being pushy. But we're kind of running out of time here and I've had way too much caffeine to pretend I'm not panicking."

Liz took one last sip of her cappuccino and stood. "Let's go look at these installations."

* * *

The sun was beginning to dip toward the horizon by the time Liz and Megan finished their final walkthrough. They stood near the entrance to the Light Forest, watching as the crew made the last adjustments. A few of the shorter pillars had been repositioned to create a more natural flow into the space, and the timing on some of the color transitions had been tweaked. Liz had been nervous about suggesting changes to the artists' work, but most of them had been receptive, even grateful for the input.

Liz's feet ached, and her voice was hoarse from talking all day, but she couldn't remember the last time she'd felt this energized.

"I don't even know how to thank you," Megan said, watching the crew work. "Like, I literally don't have words. You saw things today that I've been looking at for months. Months! And I just couldn't—" She trailed off, shaking her head.

"Sometimes you just need an outside perspective."

Megan fidgeted with one of her beaded necklaces. "So, okay, here's the thing. The festival runs for about two weeks, and I could really, really use someone—you, specifically—as like a design consultant? For the whole run? I'd pay you, obviously. A real consulting fee. I just—" She let out a breath. "I don't think I can do this without you, Liz."

Liz hesitated. "I'd have to talk to Greg."

"Of course, of course. Talk to him. Just—think about it? Please?"

Liz nodded, but even as she said she would, she had a feeling she already knew what her answer would be. She'd spent the day solving design problems on a scale she hadn't

6

worked on in years—maybe ever—and she'd loved every minute of it.

* * *

Margaret stood on the front porch of their beach house, watching as Harper and Abby walked ahead down the sidewalk toward the gate. The June evening was perfect—warm without being hot.

"Girls, wait at the corner!" she called after them.

Dave emerged from the house, pulling the door closed behind him. "They're eager."

"They've been talking about it all week," Margaret said, linking her arm through his as they started walking. "Honestly, I have too. I've been curious about this festival since I first saw the signs go up."

They caught up with the girls at the corner and continued together down the tree-lined streets, passing the familiar Victorian houses with their painted porches and manicured gardens. Other families were heading in the same direction, a slow migration toward the beach where the Luminous Festival's opening night celebration was set to begin at dusk. The shore was just one part of the festival—according to the website, there were installations scattered throughout downtown, along the promenade, and in several of the parks—but tonight, this was the main event.

"Did you see the crew setting up earlier?" Dave asked. "I drove past the beach this afternoon, and there must have been over a hundred people out there. Trucks, cranes, all kinds of equipment."

"I saw some of it from the porch," Margaret said. "They've been out there nonstop."

As they approached the main beach entrance, Margaret could already see the crowd that had gathered. Large banners proclaimed "LUMINOUS: Where Light Meets Life" in elegant

7

script, and workers in bright-blue shirts were checking wrist-bands and directing foot traffic. But it was what lay beyond the entrance that stopped her short.

Tall illuminated columns towered against the darkening sky, their colors changing and alive. Structures wrapped in strings of light dotted the landscape. Something that looked like a tunnel of luminous cloth billowed in the ocean breeze, its form constantly moving.

The salt air carried the smell of hot dogs from a vendor near the entrance, and beneath the murmur of the crowd, Margaret could hear the steady wash of waves. Children's voices rose and fell. Somewhere, a speaker played ambient music, low and dreamlike.

They joined the flow of people at the entrance, a worker scanning the barcodes on their wristbands before waving them in. Another handed them each a small pamphlet with a map of the installations. Margaret tucked hers into her pocket without looking at it. Tonight was about the beach. She wanted to experience this without a guide, to let each discovery unfold naturally.

Her sandals sank into the sand as they made their way forward.

Dozens of glowing spires rose from the sand, each one pulsing with internal light that slowly shifted through a spectrum of colors. Some reached twenty feet into the sky, slender and elegant. Others stood barely taller than a person, clustered together like saplings around their parent trees. The arrangement created natural pathways between them, drawing visitors deeper into the radiant grove.

Margaret walked through them, tilting her head back to take in their full height. The colors moved in waves, deep purple bleeding into blue, then turquoise, then green, cycling in a rhythm that felt almost like breathing. When she passed close to one, the colors shifted more rapidly, responding to her presence.

"They're interactive," Dave said, noticing the same thing. He moved his hand near one of the shorter ones and watched the light spread outward from his touch.

The girls had wandered ahead, moving through the grove and testing how the lights responded to their movement. But Margaret lingered, letting herself be surrounded by the flowing colors. The effect was disorienting and wonderful, like standing inside a kaleidoscope or beneath the northern lights.

She spotted Mary and Rob, their neighbors from down the street, near one of the taller spires, Rob with his camera out, trying to photograph the display.

"Incredible, isn't it?" Mary said when she noticed Margaret.

"I've never seen anything like it."

"Wait until you see the projections on the beach. That's supposed to be the main attraction."

They exchanged a few more words before Mary and Rob continued on their way, and Margaret rejoined Dave and the girls at the far edge of the Light Forest.

The beach itself had been transformed.

Beyond the glow of the installations, the real ocean rolled in and out, a constant backdrop to everything. Massive projections were being cast onto the beach and the shallow water, images so vivid that Margaret had to remind herself they weren't actually there. A school of silver fish darted across the ground beside her, so lifelike that a child nearby bent down to touch them. Farther out, where the sand met the water, an enormous whale glided past, its body stretching across fifty feet of shoreline.

The most stunning effects came from the mist screens—thin curtains of fog pumped up from hidden machines, creating translucent surfaces where sharks and stingrays seemed to float in midair. When the breeze shifted, the mist would waver and the creatures would shimmer and distort before reforming.

Harper and Abby lingered beside one of the taller fog displays, phones out to record a sea turtle drifting by. Margaret caught Dave's eye and smiled. This was exactly what she'd hoped the festival would be.

They continued along the installation path, passing sculptures of light-embedded fabric and a garden of mirrors that reflected the emerging stars.

The crowd began shifting toward the stage, and Margaret looked up to see what was happening.

"Something's starting," Dave said.

They collected the girls and made their way back toward the ocean. A temporary stage had been set up near the dunes, and someone was speaking into a microphone, though from this distance Margaret couldn't make out the words.

Then the lights went out.

Not just the stage lights—everything. The installations along the beach went dark simultaneously, plunging the entire festival into sudden blackness. For a moment, there was only the sound of the waves and the silence of hundreds of people holding their breath.

And then the sky erupted.

Drones, dozens of them, rose from positions along the beach, each one carrying lights that swirled in coordinated patterns. They formed shapes in the darkness: a wave cresting and breaking, a flock of birds wheeling against the stars, a spiral that expanded outward like rings on water. People gasped as the light show continued, the glowing machines filling the night sky.

Margaret watched as the drones reformed into something new, their lights shifting from white to blue to deep purple. They arranged themselves into the unmistakable shape of a lighthouse, its beam sweeping slowly across the sky. A tribute to Cape May itself.

The crowd erupted into applause as the show concluded

and the installations came back to life, their lights returning one by one until the entire beach glowed once more.

"That was unbelievable," Dave said.

Margaret nodded, still watching as the last of the drones descended back to their staging positions. Around them, families were beginning to make their way toward the exits, children wired and chattering about their favorite parts, couples walking hand in hand. She had never seen Cape May like this. She couldn't wait to see what else the festival had in store.

CHAPTER TWO

Sarah unlocked the front door of The Book Nook and stepped inside, breathing in the familiar scent of old paper and coffee that always greeted her. The floorboards creaked beneath her feet as she moved through the quiet shop, past the bay windows where she'd arranged a summer vignette—stacks of beach reads propped against driftwood, sand dollars scattered across the table, a hand-painted sign that read "Summer Escapes."

She wandered the aisles, straightening books near the entrance, adjusting the "Staff Picks" sign above a table of well-loved recommendations. She'd added touches of the season throughout—a glass vase of zinnias on the counter, vintage Cape May postcards pinned to the corkboard, a bowl of polished stones from the beach. The shop wouldn't open for another hour, but she'd wanted to come in early today. Her mind was restless, full of images from the night before.

The Luminous Festival had been unlike anything she'd ever experienced in Cape May.

She and Chris had walked through the festival installations just after sunset, staying until nearly midnight. But what had struck her most wasn't the technology or the spectacle. It was watching the artists.

Near one of the smaller pieces—a delicate arrangement of fiber optic strands woven into shapes that resembled sea grass —the artist had been standing off to the side, observing visitors interact with her work. A woman about Sarah's age with paint-stained fingers and an expression of deep satisfaction. She seemed so wholly present, so connected to what she'd created, that Sarah had felt drawn to watch her as much as the installation itself.

"She spent six months designing this piece," a volunteer had told them. "She's one of the local artists they brought on for the festival."

Six months. Sarah had thought about that the whole way home. Six months of imagining something that didn't exist and then willing it into being. Creating something from nothing but vision and determination.

The front door swung open, bringing with it a salt-tinged breeze and her part-time employee, Calvin.

"Figured you'd be here early," he said, stowing his bag. "How was the festival?"

"Incredible." Sarah leaned against the counter. "Have you been yet?"

"Going tonight with my girlfriend. She's already planned out which installations we have to see first." Calvin started his opening routine. "What was your favorite part?"

Sarah considered the question. "Watching the artists. One of them—you could just see how much of herself she'd put into it." She paused. "It made me think about what we do here. Books are art, in their own way. Stories are someone's creative vision. But we're just selling them. We're not creating anything ourselves."

Calvin raised an eyebrow. "I don't know about that. You've created this whole space, this community. People come here for more than just books."

"Maybe." Sarah looked around the shop, at the local art on the walls, the bulletin board covered with flyers for community events, the doorway to the reading room where customers lingered for hours. "But I keep thinking there's more we could do. Something that connects people to stories in a different way."

The morning passed in the usual rhythm. Customers drifted in, browsed, asked for recommendations. A mother looking for chapter books for her reluctant reader. A tourist searching for novels to fill a week's vacation. A regular named Tom who stopped by weekly for the crossword puzzle books Sarah special-ordered for him.

Around eleven, a woman Sarah didn't recognize entered the shop. She was perhaps in her early seventies, with silver hair swept up in a loose twist and tortoiseshell reading glasses. She wore a pale-yellow blouse and carried herself with posture that suggested decades of hosting dinner parties and chairing committees. Everything about her was polished—her manicured nails, her simple pearl earrings, the way she moved through the shop as though she were accustomed to being noticed.

The woman browsed slowly, running her fingers along the spines with obvious familiarity. Sarah watched her pick up a collection of Mary Oliver poems, open it to a random page, read for a moment, then close it with a small smile before moving on.

"Can I help you find something?" Sarah asked, approaching her.

The woman looked up, her eyes a pale blue behind her glasses. "I'm simply browsing, thank you. It's been quite some time since I've visited a proper bookshop. I'd forgotten how much I enjoyed it."

"Take your time. Let me know if you need anything."

Sarah returned to the counter, but she found herself glancing at the woman periodically. There was something about her—a quiet sadness, maybe, or a loneliness she couldn't quite hide.

About twenty minutes later, the woman approached with three books: the Mary Oliver collection, a novel Sarah had been recommending all summer, and a slim volume about gardens.

"Wonderful choices," Sarah said, ringing them up. "The Mary Oliver is one of my favorites."

"Mine as well." The woman nodded graciously. "I used to lead a poetry discussion group at the historical society. We read her work every spring."

"The historical society? I've been meaning to check out their programs." Sarah bagged the books. "I'm Sarah, by the way. I own the shop."

"Dorothy Hartman." The woman accepted the bag with both hands, a small nod of acknowledgment. "I kept telling myself I'd visit. I used to come to The Book Nook regularly, years ago, before the previous owners sold it. I'm afraid I fell out of the habit."

"You should come to one of our events sometime. We do author readings, book clubs, that sort of thing."

Dorothy's expression shifted slightly, a shadow of something Sarah couldn't place. "I used to adore author events. My husband and I would drive up to Philadelphia, to the larger bookstores, to hear writers speak. We hosted quite a few at our home, actually." She smoothed an invisible wrinkle from her blouse. "He passed away three years ago. I haven't entertained since."

"I'm sorry for your loss," Sarah said.

"Thank you." Dorothy adjusted her glasses. "I've been trying to venture out more lately. Trying to rejoin the world, as my daughter insists on putting it. Coming here today was part of that effort."

They talked for a few more minutes, about the shop, about Cape May, about the summer season just getting underway. Sarah found herself genuinely enjoying the conversation. Dorothy was sharp and well-read, with opinions about contemporary fiction that made Sarah laugh and nod in agreement.

"Have you been to the Luminous Festival?" Sarah asked.

"I haven't, no. I've seen the signs around town."

"You should go. I was there last night, and it was remarkable." Sarah rested her hands on the counter. "Actually, I haven't stopped thinking about it all morning. It made me want to do something like that here. Bring books and stories into the world in a new way."

Dorothy tilted her head. "What did you have in mind?"

"I'm not sure yet. Something outside, maybe? The festival is all about experiencing art in unexpected places. I keep thinking about what it would be like to do that with literature. Outdoor readings under the stars, or poetry in a garden, or..." Sarah shook her head. "I'm probably getting carried away."

But Dorothy wasn't laughing. Her face had grown thoughtful, her eyes distant.

"A garden," she repeated, almost to herself.

"Just thinking out loud," Sarah said. "Finding the right space would be the challenge. Most of the pretty outdoor spots in Cape May are either private property or too public for something intimate."

Dorothy didn't respond right away. Then she said, "I have a garden."

Sarah blinked. "I'm sorry?"

"A garden. At my house." Dorothy set her bag of books on the counter, her hands folding together in front of her. "My husband designed it over forty years ago. It was his life's work, really. He had a vision for what it could become, and he spent decades bringing it to fruition."

She stopped, and Sarah waited.

"After he died, I couldn't bear to let it go wild. I've maintained it, hired a landscaper to manage what I cannot do myself. But I rarely go out there anymore." Her voice remained steady, controlled, but Sarah could see the effort it took. "There are too many memories. Every path, every planting—Walter is everywhere in that garden."

"That must be difficult," Sarah said.

"It is. But lately I've been wondering if I've made a mistake, keeping it all to myself." Dorothy looked past Sarah, toward the window. "Walter adored that garden, but what he truly loved was sharing it. He always said a garden without visitors was just a pretty cemetery." She paused. "I think he was right."

Sarah listened, not sure where Dorothy was going with this.

"If you wanted to use it for something—for these outdoor readings you're imagining—I might be open to the idea." Dorothy lifted her chin slightly. "It would be nice to see it alive again. To have people enjoying it the way Walter always intended."

Sarah stared at her, caught off guard. "You'd really consider that?"

"I would." Dorothy reached into her purse and pulled out a small notepad and pen—a prepared gesture that suggested years of organizing events. She jotted down an address and handed it to Sarah. "Are you free this morning? I could give you a tour of the grounds."

"I'd love that. Give me an hour to get things settled here?"

"Perfect. I'll have iced tea waiting."

"Thank you, Dorothy. This is incredibly generous."

"We'll see if you still think so after you've seen the place." But Dorothy smiled as she said it.

After Dorothy left, Sarah stood behind the counter, holding the slip of paper. She pictured the kind of house Dorothy would live in—a grand old Victorian with a turret and a hidden garden.

Calvin appeared at her elbow. "You look like someone just handed you a winning lottery ticket."

Sarah laughed. "Maybe someone did." She tucked the address into her pocket. "I think I might have just found exactly the space I didn't even know I was looking for. Can you and Jenna hold things down if I head over there in an hour?"

"We've got it covered," Calvin said.

* * *

An hour later, Sarah parked on a quiet street lined with Victorian houses and double-checked the address Dorothy had given her. The house was stunning: a stately Queen Anne with a wraparound porch, painted in shades of sage and cream with burgundy accents on the trim. It was exactly the sort of place that appeared on historical walking tours. Flower boxes overflowed with petunias beneath the windows, and a brick path led from the street to the front steps, where a pair of urns held perfectly arranged topiaries.

Dorothy was waiting for her on the porch, looking every bit the proper hostess even for an informal visit.

"You found it," Dorothy said, rising to greet her. She handed Sarah a glass of iced tea—freshly brewed, from the looks of it, served in a cut crystal glass with a sprig of mint. "As promised."

"This is lovely, thank you." Sarah took a sip. It was perfect—not too sweet, with just a hint of lemon.

"Shall we?" Dorothy gestured toward the front door. "I've been looking forward to showing you the grounds."

Dorothy led her through the house, and Sarah quickly realized this wasn't just a tour—it was a carefully curated walk through decades of memories. The front sitting room had pocket doors that still worked, sliding open to reveal a dining room with a table that seated twelve. "Christmas dinner, every year," Dorothy said, running her hand along the mahogany surface. "Walter's whole family, my sister's family, sometimes neighbors who had nowhere else to go."

They passed through a sunroom with wicker furniture and faded chintz cushions. A worn leather chair sat in the corner with a reading lamp and a stack of books on the side table, as if someone had just stepped away.

"That was Walter's spot," Dorothy said. "I haven't moved anything."

Photographs covered one wall—Dorothy and Walter at various ages, at parties, on vacations, always together. Dorothy paused at one showing a younger version of herself surrounded by women holding wine glasses, all of them laughing. "We used to hold our book club meetings in here. A dozen of us, every third Thursday. I'd make cucumber sandwiches and lemon bars." She touched the frame lightly. "That feels like another lifetime."

Antique furniture filled the spaces between rooms—pieces that had likely been in the family for generations. Everything was immaculate, but there was a stillness to the house, a sense of spaces waiting to be filled again.

They stepped through French doors onto a stone patio, and Sarah stood still.

The garden spread out before her like something from a dream. Winding flagstone paths led through beds of roses, hydrangeas, and flowering shrubs she couldn't name. A pergola draped in wisteria created a shaded seating area. Farther back, she could see a small koi pond Walter must have dug himself, lily pads floating on its surface, and beyond that, a gazebo painted white with jasmine vines twisting up its supports.

"Walter's masterpiece," Dorothy said, her voice measured. "He worked on it every day after he retired. Said it was his legacy."

Sarah stepped forward, taking it all in. The garden was lush and green despite the summer heat, clearly maintained with care even if Dorothy rarely visited it. Wooden benches were positioned at intervals along the paths, ideal for sitting and reading. The gazebo had room for a few chairs, maybe a reader and a handful of listeners. She noticed details everywhere: a sundial on a pedestal, a birdbath surrounded by lavender, arbors heavy with climbing roses in shades of pink and cream.

"Walter planted those roses the year we got married," Dorothy said, following her gaze. "Forty-three years ago now. He said every anniversary he'd add a new variety."

"How many are there?" Sarah asked.

"Forty-three. One for each year. The last one—Desdemona, white with a hint of peach—he planted two months before he died." Dorothy pointed to the trellis against the back fence. "Said it reminded him of me."

Sarah felt the weight of it—the love in this garden, evident in every carefully tended bloom.

"It's perfect," Sarah breathed. "Absolutely perfect."

"You really think so?" Dorothy's voice was unexpectedly vulnerable.

"I know so." Sarah turned to face her. "I can already picture it. String lights in the trees, lanterns along the paths. Guests on the benches, an author reading near the pergola. The sound of voices and laughter mixing with the crickets."

Dorothy wasn't looking at her. She was gazing out at the garden with an expression Sarah recognized: someone trying not to feel too much.

"Are you sure about this?" Sarah asked gently. "Sharing this space with strangers? It's a big thing to offer."

Dorothy was silent for a long moment. A breeze stirred the leaves of a nearby maple, and somewhere in the garden, a bird began to sing.

"When Walter was alive," she said finally, "this garden was the heart of our social life. We hosted our daughter's wedding reception here. Anniversary parties, birthday celebrations, charity luncheons. I once had sixty people here for a midsummer garden party and hired a string quartet." She shook her head slightly. "I was a different person then. The kind of woman who kept a calendar filled months in advance and never served the same appetizer twice."

She turned to Sarah, blinking back tears.

"I've been keeping this place to myself since Walter passed, as though protecting it would somehow protect his memory. But I think I've had it wrong. Walter would want me to open these gates again. To let people in." She straightened her shoulders, and for a moment Sarah saw the formidable hostess she must have been. "Perhaps it's time I remembered who I used to be."

Sarah nodded, her throat tight.

"Books by Moonlight," Dorothy said. "That's what you should call it. Walter loved reading in the garden at night, with just the porch light to see by. He always said the words felt different in the dark. More magical."

The name settled over her like it had always been waiting.

"Books by Moonlight," she repeated. "I love it."

* * *

Higbee Beach was quiet for a summer afternoon, just a few couples strolling along the sand and a lone man with a metal detector near the dunes. Donna walked near the water's edge, letting the foam wash over her feet.

She'd gone about half a mile when she noticed a man crouched in the wet sand, sifting through it with his fingers. He had a canvas bag clipped to his belt, and every so often he'd drop something into it.

Curious, Donna slowed as she approached. "Finding anything good?"

The man looked up. He was maybe sixty, with sun-weathered skin and a faded baseball cap. "Few small shark teeth. Couple of nice Cape May diamonds." He opened his palm to show her his latest finds—two dark triangular shapes, each about the size of her thumbnail, and several smooth quartz pebbles that caught the light.

"Shark teeth? Right here on the beach?"

"All the time." He gestured toward the waterline, where the waves churned up sand and gravel. "The sediment along here is millions of years old. Back then this was all underwater— sharks, whales, all kinds of creatures. The waves erode the old layers and turn up what's been buried."

Donna knelt beside him, fascinated. "I had no idea people found things like this here."

"It's all about training your eye." He pointed to a dark shape in the sand. "See that? Looks like a pebble, but look at the edges."

She picked it up. It was small, maybe half an inch, but unmistakably triangular. The color was what struck her—dark gray, almost black.

"That's a shark tooth," the man said. "Hard to say what species from one this size—could be any number of things. But the dark color means it's been in the sediment a long time, soaking up minerals. Modern teeth are white. This one's ancient."

Donna stared at the little tooth in her fingers. Millions of years. It didn't seem possible.

"You should keep looking," he said, returning to his sifting. "The tide's going out. Good time to find things."

She walked on, but now she was scanning the sand differently. The man had told her to look for dark shapes, for anything with an unusual outline. Most of what caught her eye turned out to be shell fragments or ordinary stones, but the searching itself pulled her in. She lost track of time, moving slowly along the shore, stooping to examine anything that looked promising. She pocketed a few Cape May diamonds too —clear quartz pebbles worn smooth by the waves.

After twenty minutes, she spotted something wedged between two larger stones. Another tooth, slightly bigger than the first, with a curved shape and a distinct root at the base. She rinsed it in the surf and held it up to the light. The enamel still had a faint sheen, smooth and glossy.

Farther down the beach, she found the man again. He was talking to a woman with a bucket and a small sifting screen.

"Any luck?" he asked Donna.

She showed him the second tooth.

"Nice one. That's probably from a sand tiger. See how narrow it is, with those little side cusps?" He pointed to tiny projections flanking the main blade. "They used those for grabbing fish. Good find."

The woman with the bucket leaned over to look. "You're a natural. Took me three trips before I found my first one."

Donna ended up walking with them for a while, learning more than she'd expected. She found another tooth along the way, this one barely bigger than a grain of rice. The woman, whose name was Erica, had been fossil hunting for eight years. She showed Donna how to spot the difference between a tooth and a similarly shaped stone, how enamel reflected light differently. The man—he introduced himself as Clyde—explained about the Miocene epoch, when giant sharks called megalodons swam these waters. Their teeth could be six inches long, he said, and collectors prized them.

"That's the holy grail," Erica said. "A good megalodon tooth. I've found fragments, but never a complete one."

"I found two in fifteen years," Clyde said. "Both after the surf had been rough for a few days. Heavy waves churn everything up."

Donna spotted a flat, dark fragment with an odd honeycomb texture. She scooped it up and held it out. "What's this?"

Clyde examined it. "Could be a ray plate. Hard to say for certain, but that's what it looks like."

By the time Donna said goodbye and headed back toward the car, her pockets were heavy with finds. Three teeth total, a handful of Cape May diamonds, and the possible ray plate. She'd also taken photos of everything Erica and Clyde had found that day, for reference.

She couldn't stop thinking about it. There was so much to

learn—tidal patterns, the best conditions for searching, the different species and how to identify them. She'd lived near this beach for years and never knew any of it was here.

Dale was home when she got there, chopping onions for dinner. He looked up as she came into the kitchen.

"Good walk?"

"You're not going to believe this." Donna emptied her pockets onto the counter. "Shark teeth. Fossils. I found them right on the beach."

Dale set down his knife and picked one up, turning it in his fingers. "From around here?"

"The whole shoreline is basically an ancient ocean floor. There's a community of people who hunt for fossils—teeth, bones, you name it." She pulled out her phone to show him the photos she'd taken of Clyde and Erica's finds. "Look at what they found today."

Dale studied the images then looked back at the teeth on the counter. "We should go together sometime."

Donna grinned. "In a few days?"

"Deal."

That night, Donna stayed up late reading everything she could find about fossil hunting in the Delaware Bay area. She learned about the Miocene epoch, when giant sharks and whales swam in waters that now lay beneath New Jersey's beaches. She read about the Calvert Cliffs in Maryland, where serious collectors went, and about the local spots where amateurs had luck. She studied the difference between megalodon teeth and great white teeth, how to identify ray plates and whale ear bones, the various colors teeth could turn depending on what minerals they'd absorbed over the ages.

By the time she finally closed her laptop and climbed into bed, Dale was already asleep. But Donna lay awake for a while, her mind full of ancient oceans and prehistoric creatures, wondering what else was out there waiting to be found.

CHAPTER THREE

Bob was comparing two different grades of sandpaper when the front door of the hardware store banged open and a man he vaguely recognized came striding in. The guy was maybe forty, wearing paint-splattered jeans and a T-shirt that had seen better days, and he had the look of someone who'd just won the lottery and couldn't wait to tell the first person he saw.

"You're not going to believe this," the man announced to no one in particular. He made a beeline for the counter, where the owner was ringing up another customer. "Gilbert, wait till you hear what we found."

Gilbert looked up with the patient expression of someone who'd heard a lot of things over the years. "What'd you find, Dylan?"

Dylan Turner. That was the name. Bob recognized him from previous visits, buying supplies for what seemed like an endless renovation project on Franklin Street.

"A tunnel," Dylan said, slapping his palm on the counter. "An actual tunnel. Behind the basement wall."

The customer Gilbert had been helping paused, money in hand, suddenly interested. Bob set down the sandpaper and drifted closer.

"My contractor was tearing out the old wall at the back of the stairs," Dylan continued, the words tumbling out. "The one I told you about, with the water damage? And on the other side, there's this passageway. Five feet tall, maybe three feet wide. Goes back farther than my flashlight could reach."

"Probably an old root cellar," Gilbert said. "Lot of these Victorian houses have them."

"That's what the contractor said. But Gilbert, you should see the brickwork. It's not the same as the foundation. Different color, different size. The contractor thinks they look like 1920s manufacture—way newer than the house. Someone added it after the house was already standing." Dylan pulled out his phone and started swiping through photos. "Look at this. Look at the floor. It's packed earth, smooth as concrete. Like people walked on it. A lot."

Bob edged forward to see the screen. The photos showed exactly what Dylan had said: a narrow corridor with masonry walls, extending into darkness beyond the camera flash.

"My buddy thinks it might be from Prohibition," Dylan said. "You know, smuggling tunnels. There's always been rumors about tunnels under Cape May."

Gilbert shrugged. "Rumors, sure. But I've lived here my whole life and never come across any proof."

"Well, now you have." Dylan was practically bouncing on his heels. He noticed Bob watching and turned toward him, holding out his phone. "You want to see? It's wild."

Bob took the phone and scrolled through the photos. The tunnel looked like something more than a storage cellar— something meant to be hidden. And Dylan was right about the bricks—even in the photos, he could tell they didn't match the foundation visible at the edges of some shots.

"That's something," Bob admitted, handing the phone back.

"You should come see it in person. My wife thinks I've lost my mind, but I don't care. This is history." Dylan pocketed his phone. "Seriously, come by. I'm at 247 Franklin. The blue Victorian with the white trim."

"I might take you up on that." Bob paused. "Would it be all right if I brought my wife? She loves this kind of thing. Local history, old houses."

"The more the merrier. I'm home most afternoons, working on the renovation. Just knock."

Dylan bought a box of wood screws and left as energetically as he'd arrived, the door swinging shut behind him. Gilbert shook his head.

"That guy's been coming in here for months, talking about his renovation. Now he's got a tunnel to add to the list." He turned to Bob. "You really going to go see it?"

"I think I might," Bob said. "Judy will want to, anyway."

He paid for his sandpaper and headed home. When he told Judy about Dylan Turner and the tunnel behind the basement wall, her eyes lit up with an interest he hadn't witnessed since the lighthouse case.

"Prohibition tunnels," she said, already reaching for her jacket. "I've heard stories about those for years. Everyone talks about them, but no one's ever actually discovered one."

"Could just be a root cellar, like Gilbert said."

"Could be. But what if it isn't?" She was halfway to the door. "Are you coming?"

They drove to Franklin Street and located the house easily enough. It was a classic Cape May Victorian, three stories with a wraparound porch, painted blue with white trim just as Dylan had described. Scaffolding hugged one side where work was clearly in progress, and a dumpster in the driveway overflowed with construction debris.

Dylan answered the door before they'd finished climbing the porch steps.

"You came! Great, great. Come on in." He ushered them inside, barely pausing for introductions when Bob presented Judy. "Watch your step, we're still tearing things apart in here."

He led them through a front parlor draped in plastic sheeting and down a narrow staircase into the basement. The space was crowded with the chaos of renovation: sawhorses, power tools, stacks of lumber, buckets of joint compound. The smell of damp stone and sawdust hung in the air.

"Over here," Dylan said, guiding them around a pile of debris toward the far corner. "This is where the contractor came across it."

Judy saw it immediately. A section of the basement wall had been exposed, and where she'd expected solid stone, there was an opening. Not a gap or a crack, but a proper entryway.

"Have you been inside?" she asked.

"Just a few steps. The contractor doesn't want anyone going too far until he's sure it's stable." Dylan handed her a flashlight. "But you can see quite a bit from here."

Judy crouched at the opening and shone the light inside. Dylan's description had been accurate, but being here in person was different. The space felt deliberate—not some forgotten storage area. She noticed the ceiling had a slight arch to it, and the floor was worn into a clear path down the center. The air coming from inside was cool and damp, carrying a faint mineral smell.

Bob leaned in beside her. "You can really see the color difference. These bricks were added later."

"Exactly." Dylan's voice carried a note of vindication. "Nobody hides a coal chute behind a false wall. But a smuggling tunnel? Something you wanted to keep secret? That's a different story."

Judy swept the flashlight beam slowly across what was visible. The walls were surprisingly well constructed, laid in neat rows with consistent mortar joints. Whoever built this had known what they were doing.

She wanted to step inside, to discover where the passage led and what lay at the end. But Dylan was right to be cautious. The ceiling could be unstable, the floor could give way—there was no telling what condition the tunnel was in after being hidden away for decades.

"You should have this examined properly," Judy said, straightening up. "A historian, maybe—someone who knows old construction."

"I've been thinking the same thing," Dylan said. "I just have no idea who to call."

"Let us do some research," Bob offered. "We might be able to track down a name."

Dylan's face brightened. "That would be great. I'd love to know what this thing is." He gestured toward the tunnel. "How often does a discovery like this turn up?"

They stayed another few minutes, taking photos of the entrance and the visible stretch of tunnel. By the time they left, Judy was already thinking about the next steps.

In the car, she faced Bob. "We need to find out who owned that house in the 1920s. And whether any of the neighboring houses have similar features."

"You think there are more?"

"I think if someone went to the trouble of building one tunnel, they probably built others. And if this was really about smuggling, they'd need a network. Multiple entry points, multiple exits."

Bob nodded slowly. "So where do we start?"

"The library. County records. A tunnel like this—there has to be a paper trail somewhere."

* * *

Bob and Judy spent the rest of the afternoon at the Cape May County Library, working their way through microfilm archives and property records. It was tedious work, but Judy had always taken a certain satisfaction in research, in the slow accumulation of facts that eventually told a story.

By closing time, they'd compiled a list of properties on

Franklin Street and the surrounding blocks that had belonged to the same family during the 1920s. The Dotsons. The name kept appearing in the records: Leon Dotson, who'd owned a fishing business; his sons, Arthur and Edward, who'd inherited various holdings; a daughter, Alice, who'd moved to Philadelphia.

"Fishing operation," Bob said, studying the notes Judy had spread across their kitchen table that evening. "Good cover for bringing in more than just fish."

"My thought exactly." Judy pointed to a photocopied newspaper clipping she'd uncovered. It was from 1932, a brief obituary for Leon Dotson, describing him as a "prominent member of the community" and "devoted family man." No mention of smuggling, of course. Whatever the Dotsons had been involved in, they'd kept it quiet.

"So we have a family that owned multiple properties in the same neighborhood during Prohibition," Bob said. "And one of those properties has a tunnel hidden in the basement. What's the connection?"

"That's what we need to find out." Judy leaned back in her chair. "We should try the Historical Society tomorrow. They might be able to point us in the right direction."

"And Dylan. He'll want to know what we learned."

"Definitely. If his house was a Dotson property back then, he deserves to hear about it." She glanced down at the photocopies, at the stern face of Leon Dotson staring up from the obituary. "I have a feeling this is just the beginning."

* * *

Lisa stood in the doorway of what was supposed to be her closet, staring at the row of Nick's flannel shirts that took up three-quarters of the hanging space. His board shorts hung from a hook on the back of the door. His winter jackets, even though it was June, occupied the entire top shelf.

She'd been living at the bay house for exactly four days, and she still felt like she was staying at someone else's place.

The move itself had gone smoothly enough. Nick had helped carry everything inside, had kissed her and told her how happy he was to finally have her here. And she was happy. She was. But her boxes were still stacked in the corner of the bedroom, half-unpacked, because every time she opened a cabinet or a drawer, she found his things already there, arranged in patterns that had nothing to do with her.

His coffee mugs filled the shelf above the sink. His books lined the small bookcase in the living room. His recliner sat in the spot with the best view of the bay, positioned at exactly the angle he preferred. Even the bathroom counter held his razor, his toothbrush, his aftershave, with barely enough room for her moisturizer.

She hadn't said anything yet. It felt petty to complain about closet space when she was grateful for this, to wake up beside him every morning with the sound of the bay outside the window. But the feeling persisted—she'd walked into a life that was already complete.

"Hey." Nick appeared in the bedroom doorway. "Taking a break from unpacking?"

Lisa stepped back from the closet. "Just trying to figure out where to put things."

Nick glanced at the closet then at her. "Yeah, I guess I've kind of spread out in there." He shrugged. "We'll sort it out. Come on, I want to show you something outside."

Lisa hesitated. Part of her wanted to press the issue, to explain that it wasn't just the closet but everything—his routines, his furniture, his systems for how things worked. But Nick was already heading for the back door, and she let the moment pass.

They went out to the wooden deck that overlooked the bay. The water stretched out before them, barely rippling in the still afternoon air. A few boats moved in the distance, and closer to shore, a great blue heron stood motionless in the shallows, patient as stone.

Nick pointed toward the water's edge. "See those people out there?"

Lisa squinted against the brightness. A hundred yards down the shoreline, three figures waded through the shallow water, bent at the waist, dragging what looked like rakes through the sandy bottom.

"What are they doing?"

"Clamming. They're out there almost every day when the tide's right. I've been watching them for weeks."

One of the figures straightened up, examined something in their hand, and dropped it into a mesh bag at their waist.

"I didn't know you could do that here," Lisa said.

"Neither did I, until I moved in. Apparently this stretch of the bay is good for hard-shell clams. You need a license, but other than that, it's open to anyone."

"Have you ever tried it?"

Nick shook his head. "I've thought about it. Never got around to actually doing it." He turned to her. "You want to go talk to them?"

"Now?"

"Why not? They're right there. Worst case, they tell us to mind our own business."

Lisa held back. She'd never been the type to approach strangers, and the thought of interrupting people in the middle of their work made her self-conscious. But Nick was already moving toward the steps, an expectant look on his face.

"All right," she said. "Let's go."

They left their shoes on the deck and walked barefoot across the yard. The grass gave way to a strip of pebbly sand, and then they were wading into the bay, the water cool against Lisa's feet.

The clammers looked up as they approached. Two men and a woman, all of them somewhere in their sixties, dressed in old clothes that had clearly seen many hours in salt water. Their faces were tanned and lined from years of sun and wind.

"Afternoon," Nick called out. "We live in the house up there." He motioned toward the bay house. "Couldn't help noticing what you were doing."

The woman wiped her hands on her shorts. "Not bothering us at all. Just finishing up our limit for the day."

"I'm Nick. This is Lisa."

"Carol." She gestured to the two men. "That's Dennis, my husband, and our friend Roy."

Dennis raised a hand in greeting, while Roy just nodded and returned to his raking.

"We saw you from the deck," Lisa said. "It looks like quite an operation."

"Best spot on the bay, in my opinion." Carol adjusted the bag on her hip, which bulged with her catch. "The flats here are perfect for hard-shells. We've been coming to this area for years."

"Is it hard to learn?" Nick asked.

Carol laughed. "Nothing to it, really. You get yourself a clam rake, wade out until you're about knee-deep, and start working the bottom. The clams are usually a few inches down. You learn to feel them with the rake."

"What do you do with them all?" Lisa asked, eyeing their haul.

"Eat some, give some away to neighbors. More clams than two people can eat, even when you love them." Carol reached into her bag and pulled out a clam, holding it up. It was about two inches across, its shell gray-brown and ridged with growth lines. "This one's a good eating size—not too big, not too small. The really big ones get tough."

Dennis waded over to join them, his own bag heavy with clams. "Carol's been trying to get me to retire so we can do this full-time. I keep telling her, if I retire, I'll just end up spending more money on gear."

"We're thinking about trying it," Nick said. "Any advice for beginners?"

Carol and Dennis exchanged a look—they'd had this conversation before.

"Get a good rake," Dennis said. "And pay attention to the bottom—certain kinds of sand tell you where the clams like to be."

"Come out with us sometime," Carol offered. "We're usually here a few mornings a week. We can show you the basics."

Lisa felt a spark of interest. She'd wondered what life on the bay would look like. This was something she'd never even considered.

"We might take you up on that," she said.

They talked a while longer, learning about tides and seasons and the best spots to look. By the time they said goodbye and waded back toward shore, Lisa was hooked.

That evening, they drove into town for dinner at a new seafood place on Beach Avenue called The Catch. The interior was all reclaimed wood and nautical touches, with old photographs of fishing boats on the walls and nets draped from the ceiling.

A hostess led them to a table by the window, where they could watch the last of the daylight fading over the street outside. Lisa studied the menu.

"What about clams?" she said. "Seems appropriate, given our afternoon."

Nick smiled. "Littlenecks, cherrystones, clams casino. Take your pick."

They ordered littlenecks to start, and when the server brought them out, Lisa examined the shells with new curiosity. These were smaller than what she'd seen in Carol's bag, but the same shape, the same curved ridges.

She picked one up. "I wonder how old these are."

"A year, maybe? Year and a half?" Nick shrugged. "Puts things in perspective. Something that simple takes time."

Lisa dipped a clam in butter and ate it, tasting the brine and the sea.

"We should do it," Nick said. "Get our licenses, get the gear, go out there and see what it's like."

"You'd want to?"

"Why not? We live on the bay now. Might as well take advantage of it." He set down his fork. "Besides, it could be something we do together. Our thing."

CHAPTER FOUR

Liz pulled into the dusty lot behind the festival's operations center just after eight. She'd walked the installation sites again last night after closing, trying to see them the way a first-time visitor would, and she'd spotted an issue.

Megan was already there, pacing the length of the temporary trailer that served as festival headquarters. Her hair was pulled back with what looked like a pair of chopsticks today, and she was wearing the same clothes Liz had seen her in two days ago, now wrinkled and sporting a new stain on the hem.

"Please tell me you have good news," Megan said without preamble.

"I have concerns."

Megan groaned. "Concerns are never good. Concerns mean problems."

"The Prism Corridor." The installation was one of the festival's centerpieces—a forty-foot walkway lined with angled glass panels that split light into rainbows as visitors passed through. It had been set up on the Congress Hall lawn, facing the ocean. "The approach is all wrong. Visitors are coming from the promenade and Beach Avenue, which means they're seeing the exit first. They're walking through it backwards."

"Backwards?"

"The whole piece is designed to build. You're supposed to enter through the narrow end, where the panels are closer together, and then the space opens up as you move through. The colors shift from cool to warm, the ceiling rises—it's a journey. But the way the crowd flows right now, people are starting at the climax and ending at the introduction."

Megan's face shifted from confusion to dawning horror. "Victor is going to lose his mind."

"Victor doesn't know?"

"Victor knows everything. He's been calling me six times a day about it." Megan dropped into her chair. Her phone buzzed on the desk. She glanced at it then turned it face down without answering. "He wants us to move the entire installation. Rotate it ninety degrees so the entrance faces the hotel."

"Can we do that?"

"It's staked six feet into the ground with industrial anchors. We'd have to dig everything up, pull the anchors, restake the whole thing in a new position. That's three days minimum — and we're already open." Megan rubbed her temples. "He's threatening to pull the piece entirely if we don't fix it. He says we've 'eviscerated his artistic vision.'"

"What about redirecting foot traffic instead? Signage, barriers, maybe a roped pathway that guides people to the correct entrance?"

"I suggested that. He called it—" Megan picked up her phone and started searching. "I have it somewhere. He sent an email." She swiped through screens, frowning. "Where is it? I just had it." More swiping. "Here. Okay." She read aloud. "'A grotesque band-aid on a mortal wound. I did not spend eighteen months crafting a transcendent spatial experience to have it reduced to an amusement park queue.'"

Liz almost laughed. Almost. "He sounds like a lot."

"You have no idea. He had a piece in the Venice Biennale last year. He's been featured in ArtForum, twice. And he reminds everyone of both facts constantly." Megan lowered her voice. "He's been here almost a week and has complained about the hotel, the food, the humidity, the quality of the grass—"

"The grass?"

"Too patchy. He wanted it sodded fresh before opening." Megan threw her hands up. "It's a lawn, Liz."

The installation couldn't move, and Victor wouldn't accept a simple fix. But there had to be a middle ground. "Where is he staying? I'd like to talk to him."

Megan's eyes widened. "You would?"

"Someone needs to, and he's clearly not listening to you. Maybe a fresh voice will help."

"He's at The Virginia. But Liz, I'm warning you—he's impossible. He doesn't respond to reason. He responds to drama."

"Then I'll bring drama." Liz picked up her bag. "What room?"

Megan opened her mouth then closed it. "I... it's on the third floor. I think. Maybe the second?" She started shuffling through papers on her desk. "I wrote it down somewhere."

"I'll call ahead and confirm," Liz said.

Victor Delacroix's suite was on the third floor of Congress Hall, not The Virginia as Megan had said. Liz had called the festival office to confirm the address, and they'd redirected her. She heard him before she saw him.

She was halfway down the corridor when a muffled crash came from behind one of the doors, followed by a shriek that could have shattered crystal. A young man stood outside the room, leaning against the wall with his arms crossed and his eyes closed, as if willing himself calm.

Another crash. Something that sounded like fabric tearing.

"This is UNACCEPTABLE!" The voice was theatrical, pitched to carry. "I will not be HUMILIATED by provincial incompetence!"

The young man opened his eyes and saw Liz approaching. He was mid-twenties, with the tired look of someone who spent his days managing crises.

"You must be the design consultant," he said. "I'm Adrian. His assistant."

"Liz," she said. "Is this a bad time?"

Adrian let out a dry laugh. "There are no good times. Only degrees of bad." He tilted his head toward the door as something else hit the floor inside. "This is maybe a six. Last Tuesday was an eight."

"What's a ten?"

"I'll let you know if we survive one."

The shouting had subsided into agitated muttering. Adrian straightened up and knocked twice.

"Victor? The design consultant is here."

A pause. Then: "Send her in. And Adrian—find me a sparkling water. Still water tastes like sadness."

Adrian gave Liz a look that said good luck and headed for the stairs.

She pushed open the door and stepped inside. The sitting room had been transformed into a makeshift studio. Fabric swatches covered every surface. Sketches were pinned to the walls. A laptop played a looping video of what Liz recognized as the Prism Corridor, filmed from inside. A vase Victor must have brought with him lay shattered in the corner, its flowers scattered across the carpet, and one of his own silk pillows had been flung against the window.

And in the center of it all stood Victor Delacroix.

He was not what she'd expected. Tall and lean, mid-fifties, with silver hair that fell past his shoulders. He wore a kimono-style jacket in peacock blue over slim black pants, and his hands—currently gesturing at the laptop screen—were adorned with at least four chunky silver rings. When he turned to face her, she noticed his eyebrows first—groomed into perfect arches. His cheeks were still flushed, but his expression had already settled.

"You're not Megan," he announced.

"I'm Liz. I'm consulting on the festival's design elements."

"Design elements." He said the words like they tasted sour. "Darling, my installation is not a design element. It is a transformative spatial narrative. It is a meditation on perception and becoming. It is—" He swept his arm toward the laptop. "Being murdered."

"I saw it last night," Liz said. "You're right. The entrance is a problem."

Victor's dramatic posture softened slightly. "You noticed?"

"It's obvious. If you enter from that end, you get the payoff first. The rest is anticlimactic."

He stared at her for a long moment. "You see it. Why doesn't anyone else see it?"

"I also understand that moving the installation isn't feasible," Liz continued. "But I think there's another solution. One that might actually enhance the piece."

Victor's eyes narrowed. "I'm listening."

"The problem isn't just the entrance—it's the context. People are wandering in from the street without any preparation. There's no threshold moment, no signal that they're about to enter something special." Liz moved toward the window. "What if we created an antechamber? A transitional space that funnels visitors to the correct entrance while also setting the mood. Dark fabric panels, maybe, blocking the view of the surrounding lawn. A narrowing pathway that makes the entrance feel intentional, ceremonial. By the time they step inside, they're already primed for the experience."

Victor was silent. Then he clasped both hands to his chest.

"An antechamber," he breathed. "A threshold. Yes. Yes, I see it." He began circling the room, his rings catching the light as his hands danced through the air. "We'd need the right material. Something that absorbs light rather than reflects it.

Black velvet, perhaps, or a matte technical fabric. And the pathway—it should curve, shouldn't it? Force people to lose sight of the entrance until they're almost upon it. Build anticipation."

"Exactly. And it solves the foot traffic problem without compromising your vision. People will naturally follow the path because it's more inviting than the open approach."

Victor stopped and studied her. "You have a background in spatial design."

"Interior design. Over twenty years."

"You have an eye." He made it sound like a diagnosis. "Megan does not have an eye. Megan has spreadsheets and panic attacks. But you—" He pointed at her with one ringed finger. "You I can work with."

"I'm glad we're on the same page. But I need something from you in return."

"Oh?" One perfect eyebrow rose.

"Megan is overwhelmed. She's managing a dozen installations and twice as many egos, and she doesn't have the support she needs. If I'm going to help make this antechamber happen, I need you to stop calling her six times a day. All communication goes through me. I'll make sure your concerns are addressed, but I need you to give her room to breathe."

Victor considered this. Then he smiled—grand and performative, showing too many teeth.

"Darling, I would be delighted to never speak to that woman again."

The door opened and Adrian slipped back in, carrying a bottle of sparkling water. Victor took it without acknowledgment.

"Adrian, you heard her. Liz is our liaison now. Update the contacts."

Adrian's relief was visible.

Victor crossed to Liz and took both her hands in his. "We're going to create something magnificent. I can feel it. The antechamber will be——" He kissed his fingertips. "A revelation. Can you have drawings to me by tomorrow?"

"I'll see what I can do."

"Wonderful. Wonderful!" He released her hands and spun toward his fabric swatches. "Adrian, we need to source velvet. Black velvet, the good kind, not that cheap polyester nonsense. And find out if there's a theatrical supply company within driving distance. We may need draping hardware."

Liz took that as her cue to leave. Adrian walked her to the door.

"Thank you," he said quietly. "Sincerely. He's been unbearable since we got here."

"Is he always like this?"

Adrian's smile was weary but genuine. "This is him in a good mood."

She found Megan in the operations trailer an hour later, staring at her laptop with an expression of barely contained panic.

"Victor agreed to a compromise," Liz said. "We're building an antechamber to redirect foot traffic. He's actually excited about it."

Megan looked up. "How?"

"I spoke his language. But he wants all communication to go through me from now on."

Megan was quiet for a moment, then laughed—brittle and short. "I should be relieved, right? One less problem." She rubbed her face. "I used to be good at this, Liz. When I was at the gallery in New York, I coordinated installations for the most demanding artists in the business. I managed a team of twelve. And now I can't even keep track of which hotel Victor is staying at." She gestured at the chaos around her. "And I'm doing it all alone since my assistant quit two weeks ago."

"Show me everything," Liz said. "All of it."

They spent the next two hours going through Megan's files. By the time they finished, the scope of the disorder was clear—

missed deadlines, unanswered emails, vendor disputes that had been ignored for weeks. But so was the path forward.

They worked through the afternoon, Liz fielding calls from vendors while Megan dealt with a permitting issue that had somehow slipped through the cracks. By the time Liz headed back to her car, the sun was low and her mind full of the problems still left to solve.

* * *

Margaret was scrolling through her email when she spotted the message from the Luminous Festival volunteer coordinator—an urgent appeal for help monitoring the beach installations. Three-hour evening shifts, watching the sculptures and answering questions from the public. Tonight's assignment: the Tidal Lumina.

She found Dave in the garden and showed him her phone.

He read it over, brushing dirt from his hands. "The one that responds to the tides?"

"That's the one. They need people to answer questions, keep an eye on things."

"Sounds like a good excuse to spend the evening on the beach." He handed the phone back. "What time?"

A few hours later, they were sitting in a tent near the beach entrance for the seven o'clock orientation. Another couple was already there—Ruthie and Hank. Ruthie had close-cropped blond hair and wore a faded Blondie T-shirt under her jean jacket. Hank's forearms were covered in old Navy tattoos—anchors, a pin-up girl, something in Japanese that even he didn't know the meaning of.

"Thirty years in the Navy," he said when Margaret noticed the ink. "Most of these are from ports I barely remember."

"I told him to get them touched up," Ruthie said. "He won't."

"They're supposed to look like this. They're vintage."

43

"He thinks that makes him interesting," Ruthie said to Margaret, deadpan.

"It does. You married me."

Ruthie rolled her eyes, but she was smiling. "Best decision we ever made, retiring here. Well, second best. First was this one finally getting up the nerve to ask me out. Took him three years."

"She only says that when she wants something," Hank said. "What do you need now?"

"Nothing! I'm being nice."

"Uh huh."

The coordinator, a harried-looking man named Craig, started the session by passing around clipboards with liability waivers.

"First things first," he said, "nobody touches the equipment. I can't stress this enough. The sensors are calibrated to incredibly precise specifications. If something looks wrong, you radio it in. You do not attempt to fix it yourself."

He walked them through the basics: how the tide-response system worked, what to look for in terms of visitor safety, the protocol for emergencies.

"Most of the time, you're going to be answering questions," Craig said. "Visitors want to know how it works, who made it, whether they can take photos. The answer to the photo question is always yes."

He handed out laminated information cards with talking points about the installation. Margaret studied hers, memorizing the key facts.

"Any questions?" Craig asked.

Ruthie raised her hand. "What about emergencies? Equipment issues?"

"Radio it in. We'll send someone."

After the orientation, they walked out onto the beach to see the installation up close. It was positioned about fifty yards from the waterline, a series of interconnected light panels that rose from the sand like crystalline formations. Even unlit, the structure was striking—translucent panels in shades of amber and coral, arranged in a pattern that suggested waves frozen mid-break.

"The sensors are buried here, here, and here," Craig said, pointing to small markers in the sand. "When a wave washes over them, the lights respond. As the tide comes in and reaches more sensors, the patterns change."

Margaret crouched near one of the panels, studying how the light passed through. She could imagine how it would look once full dark settled in, glowing against the night sky, shifting in response to the rhythm of the ocean.

"It's beautiful," she said.

"Wait until you see it during a high tide after dark," Craig said. "That's when it really comes alive."

* * *

Their shift started at eight. The girls were with Paul for the night, which meant Margaret and Dave had the evening to themselves. Margaret had packed a small cooler with water and snacks, and Dave had brought the chairs.

The beach was quieter, the daytime crowds gone. Couples strolled along the shoreline, and small groups had already claimed spots near the Tidal Lumina, waiting. According to the schedule, the system would power on around eight-thirty, once night fully set in.

Margaret set up their station alongside the installation, positioning her chair where she could see both the sculpture and the waterline. Dave settled in beside her.

Ruthie and Hank took the spot next to them, having been assigned to the same shift. Ruthie had brought a thermos of sangria and a stack of plastic cups, which she started pouring before anyone asked.

"She does this everywhere," Hank said. "Beach, park, grocery store parking lot."

"It's sangria. It's civilized." Ruthie handed a cup to Margaret. "Besides, we're watching lights on a beach. This isn't a courtroom."

Dave accepted one too. "I like this already."

The first half hour passed easily. Visitors stopped to ask questions, and Margaret enjoyed the role of informal guide, pointing out the artist's subtle references to local marine life in the panel designs and fielding questions about the festival schedule.

"We've been coming to Cape May for forty years," Ruthie told Margaret. "Vacationed here every summer. Finally retired here five years ago. But I've never seen anything like this festival. It's exactly what this town needed."

"It really is," Margaret said.

"It's something to bring people together. Not just tourists, but residents too." Ruthie gestured toward the growing crowd gathering near the installation. "Look at all these faces. After all those summers, I know a lot of people in this town—but half of these folks I've never seen. Coming from all over to see this."

Around eight-thirty, the Tidal Lumina came to life.

The transformation was gradual, almost organic. First, a soft glow appeared deep within the panels. Then the colors intensified—warm ambers rippling outward from the center. The tide was just beginning to come in, and each wave that crept up the beach triggered a response in the lights, a pulse of brighter color that spread through the structure like a heartbeat.

Margaret glanced around. Children pointed and squealed. Couples held each other, mesmerized. Dave had gone still, his eyes on the lights.

As the tide came in steadily, the patterns grew more

complex. Ambers deepened to burnt orange. Coral softened to rose.

Dave nudged her arm. "Good call on this."

Margaret smiled.

A little after nine, someone down by the water shouted and pointed toward the ocean.

The moon had risen full and bright, laying a pale ribbon across the water. Margaret stood, searching. At first she saw nothing—and then a fin broke through about forty yards out, black against the moonlit sea. Another. And another.

"Sharks," Dave said, on his feet now too.

The crowd shifted, spectators edging closer to the surf to look but keeping a safe distance. A few had been wading in the shallows, but they quickly retreated to dry sand as more fins appeared. Five now. Six. Moving in loose formation.

"Sand sharks, probably," Hank said, joining them. "Used to see them all the time off the coast of Virginia. They follow the baitfish."

"They're not dangerous?" a woman nearby asked.

"Not unless you're a mullet."

The sharks cruised parallel to the shore, unhurried, their fins slicing the surface in slow arcs. The Tidal Lumina pulsed behind them, its colors reflecting off the wet sand.

Then the water erupted.

Something thrashed just beneath—a flash of silver, a spray of white water. The fins converged, cutting hard toward the commotion. More splashing. A dark shape broke the surface and disappeared.

"What is that?" a voice gasped.

The sharks were tightening now, moving faster. Whatever they were chasing was putting up a fight. Margaret could hear the slap of a tail against the water, see the churn of foam where the fins had gathered.

A child started crying. Parents pulled their kids back from

the water. Those who had been curious moments ago were now genuinely frightened.

"Is that a person?" a man shouted. "Is someone in the water?"

Margaret's stomach dropped. She reached for her radio—

"It's a fish," Hank said, his voice calm but firm. "Big one. Probably a drum or a cobia. They're hunting it."

The frenzy continued for another thirty seconds that felt much longer. Then, abruptly, a larger fin rose from the water. Much larger. It moved differently than the others—slower, more deliberate.

"Hammerhead," Hank said, leaning forward for a better look. "Haven't seen one of those in years."

The effect was immediate. The smaller sharks scattered, their fins cutting away in different directions. The hammerhead cruised through where they'd been, circled once, then headed out toward deeper water. Within a minute, every fin had vanished.

Stunned silence. Then someone laughed—a short, relieved sound—and others joined in. Applause broke out. Phones came out, too late to capture anything.

"Show's over," Hank said. "Big guy wanted the fish for himself."

"That was terrifying," Ruthie said, but she was grinning. "I loved it."

They watched for several more minutes, but the water stayed calm. The crowd began to relax, returning to their spots, chatting about what they'd seen.

Then a teenager near the surf screamed.

Not an excited scream. A real one.

Margaret was moving before she fully registered what was happening. Others were backing away from the shore, voices overlapping in confusion.

"There's a body!" someone yelled. "Something washed up!"

Margaret's heart hammered as she pushed through the

small group that had formed. In the dim light, she could see something at the edge of the surf—pale, human-sized, face-down in the shallow water. A wave pushed it higher onto the sand.

She grabbed her radio. "This is the volunteer station at Tidal Lumina. We have a possible—"

Then she got closer.

The shape was too stiff. Too smooth. And where the head met the shoulders, there was a hinge.

"It's a dummy," she said, half to herself. Then louder: "Everyone, it's okay. It's a CPR dummy."

She crouched down and pulled it farther up the beach. Sure enough—a rubber training mannequin, the kind they used in first aid classes. Torso, head, no arms or legs. Faded and waterlogged, like it had been in the ocean for a while.

"Must have fallen off a boat," Dave said. "Coast Guard, maybe. Some kind of training exercise."

The tension dissolved. Nervous laughter spread. A few people took photos. The teenager who'd screamed was bright red, her friends already teasing her.

Hank wandered over. "Seen worse wash up in the Pacific," he said, nudging the dummy with his foot. "At least this one's not a refrigerator."

"A refrigerator?" Margaret asked.

"Don't ask."

Ruthie appeared beside them. "That was quick thinking with the radio."

"I almost called in a body," Margaret said, still catching her breath. "Can you imagine?"

"Thankfully it wasn't real." Ruthie clinked her cup against Margaret's. "To the weirdest volunteer shift I've ever had."

"It's only our first one," Dave said.

"Then it's going to be an interesting week."

They dragged the dummy above the tide line and radioed

Craig to arrange pickup. Onlookers lingered to take selfies with it.

"That," Dave said to Margaret as they walked back to their station, "was not what I expected from volunteer work."

"Better or worse?"

He considered. "Better. Definitely better."

They stayed until midnight, handing off to the overnight security who would watch the installation until dawn. Walking back to the house, Margaret realized she was already looking forward to the next shift.

CHAPTER FIVE

The fog had rolled in sometime before dawn, and Higbee Beach had disappeared into the mist. Donna could taste the salt in the air as she and Dale made their way down the sandy path toward the water.

"Stay close," she said, only half-joking. "I don't want to lose you out there."

The dune grass on either side appeared and disappeared like ghosts. The usual markers she used to orient herself were gone, swallowed by the fog. No horizon line, no distant houses, no other beachgoers. Just the two of them.

"This is a little eerie," Dale admitted.

"I know. I love it."

They reached the beach and turned right, heading toward the stretch where Donna had found her first teeth. The sand was damp beneath their feet, packed hard by the retreating tide. Every few steps, the fog would thin just enough to reveal a glimpse of the waterline before closing in again.

Donna knelt at the water's edge, scanning the sand the way Clyde had taught her. Dark shapes against the lighter background. Unusual outlines. Anything that didn't quite fit.

"What am I looking for?" Dale asked, crouching beside her.

"Triangles, mostly. The teeth are usually dark, almost black. They absorb minerals from the sediment over millions of years." She pointed to a cluster of pebbles. "See how those are all rounded? That's just erosion. But if you find something with a point, with edges that look intentional, that's worth picking up."

Neither of them spoke for a while, the fog creating a strange intimacy around them. Donna could hear the soft scrape of fingers through the sand, the quiet push and pull of the tide. The rest of the world had ceased to exist.

She found her first tooth within ten minutes, a small dark triangle no bigger than her pinky nail. She rinsed it in the shallow water and held it up.

"Got one."

Dale leaned over to look. "That's it? That's a shark tooth?"

"Probably sand tiger, based on the shape. See how narrow it is?"

"I was expecting something bigger."

"Keep looking. Bigger ones are out here too."

They moved farther down the beach, stopping every few yards to sift through the dark bands of shell and sediment the tide had left behind. Dale found a handful of Cape May diamonds, the clear quartz pebbles that caught even the dim light filtering through the fog. Donna picked up a dozen likely candidates that turned out to be ordinary pebbles before she spotted another tooth, this one even smaller than the first.

A figure materialized out of the mist ahead of them.

Donna's heart jumped before her brain caught up. The shape resolved into a familiar silhouette: baseball cap, mesh bag at the hip, the easy pace of a regular.

"Clyde?"

The figure turned, and she recognized the lined, tanned face from her first visit. He relaxed when he saw her.

"Well, look who's back." He ambled toward them, his water

shoes leaving prints in the wet sand. "Brought reinforcements this time."

"This is my husband, Dale. Dale, this is Clyde. He's the one who taught me the basics."

Dale extended his hand. "Good to meet you. Donna hasn't stopped talking about shark teeth since she got home last time."

Clyde's handshake was firm. "Once you find your first one, you're hooked." He glanced at the fog surrounding them. "Interesting day to be out here."

"Is it bad for hunting?" Donna asked.

"Depends on how you look at it. Can't see what's coming, which some people don't like. But the fog keeps the crowds away." He gestured vaguely toward the invisible parking lot. "Usually by this hour you've got a dozen people working this stretch. Today it's just us." He paused. "Well, us and one other."

The way he said it made Donna look up. "Someone else is out here?"

Something in Clyde's voice changed. "Fellow named Garret. Professional collector. Been working the Jersey beaches for years." He started walking, and Donna and Dale fell into step beside him. "He's got all the gear. Sifting screens, collecting bags, the works. Drives down from Trenton every few weeks and strips a section clean."

"Is that legal?" Dale asked.

"Legal enough. Public beach, anyone can hunt here. But there's a code, you know? Most of us, we take what we find and leave some for the next person. Garret..." Clyde shook his head. "Garret doesn't believe in leaving anything behind."

They walked in silence for a moment, the fog pressing in around them.

"Does he sell what he finds?"

"Online mostly. Got a website, the whole operation. Charges hundreds for the good stuff." Clyde's voice carried a note of disgust. "Nothing wrong with selling, necessarily. But the way he does it, treating every beach like his personal inventory, pushing other collectors out of the good spots..." He trailed off. "Just rubs me wrong."

As if summoned by the conversation, someone else appeared ahead of them through the mist. This one was different from Clyde, moving with purpose rather than patience. As he drew closer, Donna could make out the details: a man in his forties with a shaved head who had the look of someone who'd spent serious money at an outdoor store. He carried a large sifting screen under one arm. A canvas bag hung from his shoulder, clearly heavy with whatever he'd already collected.

Clyde slowed but didn't stop. "Garret."

The man barely glanced at them. "Clyde." His eyes stayed on the sand as he scanned the gravel line. "Good day for hunting. Fog keeps the tourists home."

"That's what I was telling these folks."

Now Garret looked up, his eyes moving over Donna and Dale with quick assessment. She felt sized up and dismissed.

"Beginners?" He didn't wait for an answer. "Word of advice: stick to the upper beach. The real prizes are down by the waterline, and you need to know what you're doing to score there." He returned his attention to the sand. "Lot of people come out here thinking they'll find a megalodon on their first try. Doesn't work like that."

"We're not looking for megalodons," Donna said, keeping her voice even. "Just enjoying the hunt."

Garret snorted. "That's what everyone says. Then they find one small tooth and think they're experts." He crouched suddenly, scooping up a handful of gravel and sifting it through his fingers. He plucked out a dark object, examined it briefly, and dropped it into his bag. "Most people don't have the patience for this. Or the eye."

"Some of us manage," Clyde said.

Garret's eyes cut to him. "Some of you pick through what's

left over. Big difference." He shouldered his bag and continued down the beach, his gaze fixed on the sand. "Good luck out there. You'll need it."

They watched him disappear into the fog.

"Charming," Dale said.

"That's Garret." Clyde set off again, angling away from the direction the other man had gone. "Don't let him get to you. He's been doing this longer than most, and he thinks that gives him ownership of every beach on the coast."

"Does he always hunt here?" Donna looked back.

"Higbee's one of his regular spots. But he moves around. Follows the erosion, the storm patterns. Wherever the best stuff is washing up, that's where you'll find him." Clyde paused at a section of beach where the gravel seemed denser, more concentrated. "Here's a good spot. The recent tides have been pushing material up from the deeper layers."

They spread out, each taking a section. The fog had thinned slightly, enough that Donna could see maybe thirty feet in either direction. The waves sounded closer now, louder.

She worked methodically, sifting through handfuls of sand and pebbles, looking for the distinctive shapes she'd learned to recognize. She found a smooth piece of quartz, then a fragment of shell, then something that made her pause.

"Dale, look at this."

He came over, and she showed him her find. It was pale, almost white, with a porous texture unlike anything else on the beach. About three inches long, curved, with what looked like attachment points at both ends.

"Bone?" Dale asked.

"I think so."

Clyde appeared at her elbow, his expression curious. He took the piece from her and turned it in his fingers, examining it from different angles.

"Nice find. That's a vertebra, I'd say. Fish or small marine mammal."

"Really? Like a dolphin?"

"Could be. Could be seal, could be porpoise. Hard to say without a closer look." Clyde handed it back. "Keep it. That's a good one."

Encouraged, they continued searching. The fog ebbed and flowed around them, sometimes lifting enough to reveal a wider expanse of shoreline, sometimes closing in until they could barely see each other. Donna lost track of time, absorbed in the hunt. She collected more of the clear stones and a few broken shells, but no more teeth. The hunting was slower than she'd expected.

Dale straightened up, holding something in his palm. "Hey, what's this?"

She crossed to him, Clyde following. Dale held out a piece of bone larger than anything they'd found so far. Maybe five inches long, thick and heavy.

Clyde turned it over in his hands. "Whale vertebra. That's a keeper—whale bone doesn't turn up every day."

Dale grinned, weighing it in his hand. "Not bad for my first real outing."

The next hour passed quickly. Dale found a tooth, his first, and Donna added a few more Cape May diamonds to her collection. The fog began to lift around midmorning, the gray thinning to reveal patches of blue sky. Other beachcombers had started to appear, drawn out by the improving weather. Donna spotted Garret in the distance, still working the water-line, his bag bulging with the morning's haul.

"We should head out," Dale said. "I've got some things to take care of this afternoon."

They said goodbye to Clyde, who planned to stay a while longer. He gave them tips on identifying what they'd found and recommended some websites where they could learn more about local fossils.

"You two have good instincts," he said as they parted. "Keep at it. The really big finds, the ones that end up in museums, they don't go to the people with the best equipment. They go to the people who put in the time."

Walking back to the car, Donna mentally cataloged their haul. Two small teeth for her, one for Dale, a handful of Cape May diamonds between them, her vertebra fragment, and Dale's whale bone. Not a huge haul, but enough to keep her interested.

She thought about what Clyde had said. The patience required, the hours of searching for every small discovery. It wasn't about the end result so much as the process, the meditation of it.

"That was fun," Dale said.

"Even with Garret?"

"Especially with Garret." He smiled. "Now I want to get good enough to prove him wrong."

* * *

Sarah arrived at Dorothy's house an hour before the event was scheduled to begin. She'd kept it simple: a cooler of lemonade and iced tea in the trunk, a box of books to sell, and a couple of balloons to tie to the front gate so people would know which house. The whole point of Books by Moonlight was to be casual—bring a chair or a blanket, bring a dish to share if you wanted, settle into the garden and enjoy an evening with fellow book lovers. A local author, Julia Reeves, had agreed to do a short reading at some point, but mostly it was about community.

The June evening was perfect for an outdoor gathering, a light breeze carrying the scent of someone's backyard grill. She paused, taking in the view of the Victorian house with its wraparound porch and manicured gardens.

This was really happening. Books by Moonlight. The name Dorothy had suggested, now brought to life in her extraordinary garden.

She tied the balloons to the front gate then headed around the side of the house toward the back garden. The path was lined with solar lanterns, but as Sarah rounded the corner, she came to a halt.

The garden had been transformed.

Not in any way Sarah had anticipated. She'd pictured people spreading blankets on the lawn, clustering on benches, drifting along the paths with glasses of wine. Instead, the garden looked like a society luncheon from 1962. Rows of white wooden chairs faced a podium—an actual podium, with a microphone—arranged in rigid formation like a lecture hall. Velvet ropes sectioned off the first two rows, brass signs marking them "Reserved." A harpist in a black gown sat near the roses, already plucking away at something classical. And at the garden's entrance, a photographer had set up a backdrop, apparently to take formal portraits of arriving guests.

Dorothy emerged from the house, carrying a silver tray. She wore a soft rose dress with pearls, her hair arranged more elaborately than Sarah had ever seen it.

"Sarah! You're early. Wonderful. I wanted to show you the improvements I made."

"Improvements?"

"I realized you hadn't arranged for proper seating, so I took care of it." Dorothy set the tray on a linen-draped table that hadn't been there before. "I consulted with my friend Helen, who does feng shui, and she helped me position everything. The chairs face east, toward the rising moon. It creates a more receptive atmosphere for the audience."

Sarah looked at the rows of chairs, the podium, the harpist. It was impressive, undeniably. But it looked more like a charity gala than a casual evening in the garden.

"It's beautiful," she said carefully. "But Dorothy, this isn't what I described to people. They're expecting something... different."

"Different how?"

"More relaxed. Informal."

Dorothy waved a hand and straightened one of the velvet ropes. "Nonsense. Everyone appreciates an upgrade. Trust me, I've hosted hundreds of events."

Sarah found a spot near the gate to set up her book table—visible, accessible, where guests could browse on their way in or out. She'd just finished arranging her display when Dorothy appeared with an armload of items.

"I thought we could make this more inviting." Dorothy was already setting things down—a leather guest book, a stack of garden tour brochures, a framed photo of Walter beside his prize roses, another of the garden in full bloom. "People love to see what they're supporting."

"But this is the book table—"

"And now it tells a story." Dorothy positioned the photo of Walter front and center. Sarah's books got pushed to the edges, half-hidden behind the brochures. "Much better."

Sarah stared at her display, now barely visible among the memorial to Walter and his garden. She opened her mouth to argue, but a car pulled into the driveway. Then another. People were arriving.

"Oh, that must be the Woodmans," Dorothy said, brightening, already moving toward the gate to greet her guests. "Don't worry about a thing, Sarah. I have it all under control."

It wasn't the Woodmans.

Sarah stood in the transformed garden and felt the evening slipping away from her before it had even begun.

The next forty minutes were chaos.

Sarah's guests arrived in flip-flops and shorts, tank tops and sundresses, a few carrying hoodies in case the evening turned cool. Several had folding beach chairs under their arms. One couple carried a blanket and a picnic basket. A woman showed up with a bottle of wine and a wedge of brie, clearly expecting the potluck Sarah had described. They stopped at the garden entrance, blinking at the velvet ropes and the photographer, then looked down at their casual clothes with visible confusion.

The photographer gestured toward the backdrop. "Portrait before you enter?"

A man in cargo shorts and a faded Wildwood T-shirt stared at him. "I'm good, thanks."

"It's complimentary. For the guest book."

"I'm... really good."

The photographer shrugged and checked his phone as guest after guest waved him off, sidling past the backdrop like it might bite them.

Dorothy watched the arrivals, her smile frozen in place. For a moment, something crossed her face—not quite horror, but close.

"I see what you meant about casual," Dorothy murmured as Sarah passed.

Then Dorothy's guests began arriving—the Woodmans, the Lowensteins, the Hendricks—and Sarah quickly realized that most of them had no idea what Books by Moonlight actually was. They'd been invited by Dorothy, presumably with descriptions that emphasized the garden party aspect rather than the literary one. Sarah overheard one woman telling another that she expected canapes and wine, not a book reading. Another asked where the string quartet was setting up.

The refreshment table was a study in contrasts. Sarah's guests had brought potluck contributions—a caprese salad, hummus with pita, a fruit tray, brownies still warm from the oven. But Dorothy had prepared food herself, and it was clear her entertaining style hadn't evolved since 1975. There were finger sandwiches with fillings Sarah couldn't identify, small aspic molds trembling on a silver platter, a cheese ball crusted in chopped walnuts, and something that appeared to be liver pâté molded into the shape of a pineapple. A towering crudité tree dominated one end of the table—vegetables speared onto a styrofoam cone covered in foil. And at the center, a punch bowl filled with something pink that had visible chunks of fruit floating in it.

Guests clustered around the brownies and caprese. The aspic sat untouched.

Dorothy noticed. Within seconds she was rearranging the table, sliding the potluck dishes to the far end and positioning her own food prominently.

"There," she said, repositioning the punch ladle. "That's how it should look."

Sarah watched the caprese salad get pushed behind the crudité tree and said nothing.

"I made my mother's famous reception punch," Dorothy announced proudly. "It's been a hit at every party I've ever thrown."

Sarah took a polite sip and immediately understood why the bowl was still mostly full. The punch was aggressively sweet, with an undertone of artificial cherry that clashed with the bits of canned pineapple bobbing on the surface.

"Interesting," she managed.

"I wanted to contribute," Dorothy said, smoothing the tablecloth. "You've done so much work, and I wanted you to know how much this means to me."

"It all looks very... festive," Sarah said.

More guests arrived, including Julia herself. She took one look at the formal seating arrangement and her face shifted.

"This is different from what we discussed," she said quietly to Sarah.

"I know. I'm so sorry. The homeowner had some last-minute ideas."

"The homeowner being the woman guarding the velvet ropes?"

"That's Dorothy, yes."

"We'll make it work." Julia squeezed Sarah's arm. "Worst case, I'll just talk louder than the harpist."

One of her regulars, a young woman named Gabi who

taught yoga at the studio on Washington Street, approached Sarah with concern in her eyes.

"Is this the right place? I thought it was going to be more..."

"Casual?" Sarah finished. "It was supposed to be. Dorothy had other ideas."

Gabi glanced at the aspic tray. "Is that jello with things inside it?"

"Don't ask."

"I wasn't going to eat it anyway."

Sarah started to direct Gabi toward the back of the garden where she could set up her beach chair, but Dorothy materialized beside them.

"Oh no, dear, the seating is up front." Dorothy gestured toward the rigid rows of white chairs. "We have a system."

"She brought her own chair," Sarah said. "I told people they could—"

"The chairs are already arranged." Dorothy's smile didn't waver, but her tone left no room for argument. "We can't have people scattered all over the lawn. It would look chaotic."

Sarah felt her face flush. Gabi looked between them, clearly uncomfortable.

"It's fine," Gabi said quickly. "I'll just... find a spot."

Gabi retreated toward the rear of the lawn, folding chair still under her arm. Sarah's stomach knotted. This was supposed to be her event.

Sarah caught up with Dorothy by the punch bowl.

"Dorothy, can we talk for a minute? I think we need to—"

"Not now, dear. We have guests." Dorothy patted her arm without slowing down. "We'll chat after."

She was gone before Sarah could respond, greeting a couple who'd just arrived through the gate, leaving Sarah standing alone with her unfinished sentence.

More Book Nook regulars filtered in, clustering in the last

rows of chairs, out of place among Dorothy's society friends. Sarah could feel the divide widening.

Dorothy was back, this time with a woman in tow.

"Sarah, this is Peggy Van Dorn. Peggy is the president of the Cape May Horticulture Club. Peggy, this is Sarah, the bookshop owner I told you about."

Peggy Van Dorn had perfectly coiffed blond hair and a designer dress that probably cost more than Sarah's monthly rent. She looked Sarah up and down.

"How nice that you're doing something with Dorothy's garden," Peggy said. "It's been such a shame, seeing it closed off all these years." Peggy's attention had already shifted. "Oh, there's Helen. I must say hello. Lovely to meet you, Sarah."

She swept off toward a group of women near the refreshments.

The crowd had grown to nearly forty people, far more than Sarah had anticipated. Dorothy's guests seemed to outnumber Sarah's. The garden, for all its charm, was starting to feel crowded.

A bell chimed—Peggy Van Dorn's contribution to the evening. She'd appointed herself timekeeper and was now standing near the gazebo, summoning everyone to their seats.

"The reading is about to begin," she announced, loud enough to be heard across the entire garden. "Please take your assigned seats."

Sarah headed for the front of the garden, where Peggy was still directing people to their seats with the efficiency of an air traffic controller.

Julia was waiting near the gazebo, her book of essays in hand. She gave Sarah an encouraging nod.

"Ready?" Sarah asked.

"Born ready."

Sarah stepped up to the small platform they'd set up for the reading. The crowd had settled into their seats, though with considerable grumbling about the arrangement. Dorothy's friends occupied the front rows with their name cards, while the Book Nook subscribers had squeezed into the back wherever they could find space.

"Good evening, everyone," Sarah began. "Welcome to the first ever Books by Moonlight. We're thrilled to have you here in this extraordinary garden, generously opened to us by Dorothy Hartman."

She paused for applause, which came enthusiastically from Dorothy's contingent and politely from everyone else.

"Tonight's reader is Julia Reeves, whose collection Life at the Water's Edge has been called 'a love letter to the Jersey Shore.' Please join me in welcoming Julia."

Julia stepped up, and Sarah retreated to the side of the garden. From here she could see the whole crowd.

The reading started well. Julia had a strong voice and a natural presence, and her essays were moving. Stories of fishermen and boardwalk vendors, of storms and sunrises, of the light on the water at dawn. The audience was quiet, attentive.

Dorothy had positioned herself at the end of the front row, and she took her role as hostess seriously. When someone's chair creaked, she turned with a sharp look. When a man in the back coughed, she held a finger to her lips. When two of Sarah's regulars leaned together to whisper something—probably about how beautiful the garden was—Dorothy's "Shhh!" cut across the space like a whip crack.

Sarah observed this with growing unease. The audience wasn't being disruptive. They were being human.

Then Peggy started whispering.

At first it was barely audible, just a murmur to the woman beside her. But as Julia continued reading, Peggy's commentary grew louder. Sarah caught fragments: "...not really literature, is it..." and "...anyone could write this..." and "...I preferred the garden party aspect myself..."

Julia paused mid-sentence, her rhythm thrown.

Peggy didn't seem to notice. She was deep in conversation

now with two other women, their voices creating a constant undercurrent beneath Julia's words.

Sarah's hands tightened at her sides. She'd dealt with difficult customers at the bookshop, people who talked on their phones or let their children run wild. But this was different. This was deliberate rudeness, dressed up as sophisticated indifference.

She was about to intervene when Dorothy beat her to it.

"Peggy." Dorothy's voice cut through the garden like ice. "The author is reading."

Peggy looked up, startled. "I was just saying to Helen that the garden looks lovely."

"Then say it quietly, or say it later." Dorothy's composure was absolute. "We didn't invite Ms. Reeves here to be background noise."

The silence that followed was total.

Peggy went red. Her mouth opened, then closed. Sarah thought she might argue. Then she nodded stiffly and folded her hands in her lap.

"Thank you," Dorothy said, and gestured for Julia to continue.

The reading resumed, and this time no one interrupted. Julia finished her selection to genuine applause, and Sarah noticed that several of the Book Nook subscribers had moved closer, drawn in by the quality of the writing.

The mingling period that followed should have been the heart of the event—a chance for readers to meet, talk about books, connect. But the harpist had resumed playing through a small speaker, and Dorothy had apparently instructed her to turn up the volume. The arpeggios echoed off the garden walls, making normal conversation impossible. Sarah watched guests lean in and cup their ears, shouting to be heard, then give up and drift apart.

She found Dorothy near the refreshment table, refilling the punch bowl from a crystal pitcher.

"Dorothy, the harp is a bit loud. People can't really talk."

"It creates atmosphere," Dorothy said. "Background music is essential for a proper garden party."

"But people want to discuss the reading. That's the whole point of—"

"Sarah." Dorothy's tone was patient but final. "I know what I'm doing."

Sarah bit back her response and walked away. Across the lawn, she saw Gabi and two other Book Nook regulars heading for the gate, their early departure unmistakable.

Later, Dorothy found her near the back fence. "Peggy can be difficult," she said. "I wasn't going to let her ruin the reading."

"I appreciate it," Sarah said. "I wasn't sure how to address it without making things worse."

"Peggy and I have known each other for thirty years. She's used to being the center of attention. Sometimes she needs reminding that not every gathering is about her."

"Still. Thank you."

"This is my garden," Dorothy said simply. "My husband's garden. I won't have it disrespected."

Sarah didn't know what to say to that. The garden was magical—she couldn't deny it. The string lights glowed softly over the roses and paths, the moon rising above the trees. But half her regulars had already left, and the harp was still drowning out conversation.

It wasn't what she'd planned. Not even close.

The evening wound down gradually, guests departing in small groups. Julia had sold out her entire stock and was accepting orders for more. Sarah's own books had barely moved—people kept stopping at the table to admire the photos of Walter's garden instead. Dorothy's society friends and Sarah's casual bookshop regulars had stayed on opposite sides of the garden all night, barely exchanging a word.

Sarah loaded her cooler into the car and sat behind the

wheel, exhausted. The event had happened. She wasn't sure she could call it a success.

As she pulled away from the curb, she couldn't help wondering: if they did this again, would Dorothy be able to step back? Or would every Books by Moonlight become a battle for control?

She didn't have an answer. Not yet.

CHAPTER SIX

Judy rang the doorbell and stepped back beside Bob on the narrow front porch. The house on Hughes Street was a modest Victorian, smaller than most in the historic district but meticulously maintained. Window boxes overflowed with red geraniums, and the porch railings had been painted so recently that Judy caught the lingering smell of wet paint.

The woman who answered the door was small and white-haired, with eyes that assessed them briefly before softening.

"Mrs. Wright?" Judy extended her hand. "I'm Judy. We spoke on the phone yesterday."

"Gladys." The woman's handshake was surprisingly firm. "And you must be Bob, the husband. Come in, come in. I've got tea on."

The interior of the house was frozen somewhere around 1985. Floral wallpaper lined the entryway, and the living room featured a matching sofa and loveseat in dusty rose, sheathed in plastic covers, positioned around a glass-topped coffee table. Framed photographs covered nearly every surface, generations of faces staring out from silver frames.

Gladys Wright was eighty-nine years old, according to the research Judy had done through the Historical Society's membership records. Her maiden name had been Brocade, and her grandfather Thomas Brocade had owned three properties on Franklin Street during the 1920s, including the one directly adjacent to Dylan Turner's house.

"Sit, sit." Gladys gestured toward the sofa while she lowered herself into a wingback chair that had clearly been hers for decades. "Now, you said on the phone this was about the old neighborhood. Something about a tunnel."

"That's right." Judy settled onto the sofa—plastic crinkling beneath her—with Bob beside her, accepting cups of tea from the tray Gladys had prepared before they arrived. "A friend of ours is renovating a house on Franklin Street. He found a passageway hidden behind his basement wall."

Gladys's expression didn't change, but her gaze sharpened. "Hidden, you say."

"Behind a false wall. The brickwork doesn't match the original foundation. It looks like it was added sometime in the 1920s."

"And you think this has something to do with my family because...?"

"Because your grandfather owned the property next door during that period," Bob said. "And from what we've gathered, several Brocade properties were in that same block."

Gladys was quiet for a long moment. She picked up her own tea cup and held it without drinking, her eyes on some point beyond the window.

"You're not the first to come asking about this," she said finally. "Back in the seventies, a man from the state historical commission came around. Wanted to know about Prohibition-era smuggling routes along the coast. I told him what I'm going to tell you. I don't know anything about any tunnels."

Judy recognized the careful phrasing. Not "there were no tunnels." Not "I've never heard of them." Just a declaration of personal ignorance that left all doors open.

"Mrs. Wright, we're not here to cause trouble for anyone,"

Judy said. "We're just curious. The house is being renovated, and the owner wants to understand what he's found."

"Curious." Gladys set her cup down with a quiet click against the saucer. "Curiosity is how trouble starts, in my experience."

"We understand this might be a sensitive subject," Bob said. "Family history often is."

That seemed to reach her. Gladys's shoulders relaxed slightly.

"My grandfather was a practical man," she said. "He did what he had to do to support his family during hard times. That's all I know, and that's all I'll say about him directly." She took a breath. "But I can tell you this. The Brocades looked out for each other. Always have. And back in those days, looking out for each other sometimes meant making certain... arrangements."

"Arrangements," Judy repeated.

"The basements were connected for a reason." Gladys met her eyes directly for the first time. "That's not a secret I'm revealing. It's something everyone in the family knew. We just don't talk about it with outsiders."

"Do you know how many properties were connected?" Judy asked.

"I was a child when I heard these stories. My grandmother told them to me when she thought I was old enough to understand. But even she was vague about the details. She said it was safer not to know too much." Gladys picked up her tea again, and this time she drank. "What I remember is that there were at least three houses involved. Maybe four. And the connections weren't just for moving goods. They were for moving people too. For safety, when the authorities came looking."

Bob leaned forward. "Do you know which properties specifically?"

"The house your friend is renovating, certainly. The one next door, which my grandfather owned. There was a third on the corner that belonged to a cousin, but it was torn down in the fifties." Her brow furrowed. "And there were rumors it went beyond just the houses. But that I never understood clearly."

If the tunnel in Dylan's basement connected to the neighboring property, and that property connected to others, they might be looking at an entire network.

"Is that house still in your family?" she asked.

Gladys shook her head. "Sold in 1968. My father needed the money for medical bills. It's changed hands several times since then."

"Do you know who owns it now?"

"Some young couple, I think. They painted it that awful shade of yellow last year." Gladys's mouth twitched in disapproval. "The original color was blue. Brocade blue, we called it."

"How would you feel about us investigating further?" Bob asked. "We'd want to contact the current owners, see if there's anything in their basement."

Gladys didn't answer right away. The clock on the mantel ticked into the silence.

"I spent my whole life protecting this family's reputation," she said at last. "My grandfather wasn't a criminal. He was a businessman who operated in an impossible environment. Prohibition was foolish from the start, and everyone knew it. The people who kept the liquor flowing were performing a public service, as far as most folks were concerned."

"We're not here to judge," Judy said.

"No, but others might." Gladys's eyes hardened. "If you're going to dig into this, I want something from you. I want to know what you find. Not to stop you. But so I can prepare, if there's anything that might come out that reflects poorly on my family."

"That's fair," Bob said.

"There's one more thing." Gladys rose from her chair with

careful movements. She crossed to an antique secretary desk in the corner and opened a drawer. "If you're serious about this, you should talk to the people at the Cape May Historical Society. There's a woman there, Fran Martino. She's been researching Prohibition-era Cape May for years. Tell her I sent you."

She returned with a small photograph, edges yellowed with age. It showed a group of men standing in front of a storefront, their faces serious, their clothes marking them as working class.

"That's my grandfather." Gladys pointed to a man on the far right. "Thomas Brocade. And the man beside him is Leon Dotson."

Judy's breath caught. Dotson. The same family that had owned Dylan's house.

"They were partners?" she asked.

"They were friends. Good friends, from what I understand. Whatever business they conducted together, they kept it between themselves." Gladys took the photograph back and studied it for a moment before returning it to the drawer. "That's all I have for you. I hope you find what you're looking for. But be careful what doors you open. Some of them were closed for good reason."

* * *

Fran Martino was waiting for them in the lobby of the Cape May Historical Society two hours later, a compact woman with dark curly hair and a tote bag covered in buttons from various historical conferences.

"Judy and Bob?" She shook their hands with enthusiasm. "Gladys called ahead. Said you'd found something interesting."

"That's one way to put it," Bob said.

Fran led them through the Colonial House's front rooms, past period furnishings and old portraits on the walls, toward a back office cluttered with books, papers, and cardboard boxes labeled with dates and locations. A large map of Cape May hung on one wall, dotted with colored pins.

"I've been researching Prohibition-era Cape May for fifteen years," Fran said, clearing a stack of files off two chairs so they could sit. "Most people think of the big operations, the rum runners coming up from the Caribbean, the boats unloading on the beaches. But there was a whole network of smaller operations too. Local people moving local product."

"That's what we've been finding," Judy said. She pulled out the photographs they'd taken at Dylan's house. "This is the tunnel. Or passage, or whatever you want to call it."

Fran took the photos and studied them.

"The brickwork is distinctive," she said. "See how the mortar's laid? That's a technique that was common in the twenties, but it fell out of fashion by the thirties. And these bricks have a particular color that comes from a kiln that used to operate in Cape May Court House." She set the photos down. "I'd say your friend's tunnel was built sometime between 1922 and 1928. Right in the middle of Prohibition."

"Gladys Wright suggested the basements in that neighborhood were connected," Judy said. "Multiple properties linked together."

"That matches what I've found in the records." Fran crossed to her map and pointed to a section of Franklin Street. "The Brocade family owned property here, here, and here. The Dotsons owned this one and this one. And there was a third family, the Kellermans, who had a house on the corner." She stepped back, surveying the pins. "But I've always suspected there's more. These are just the ones I can document."

"All of them connected?" Bob asked.

"That's the question, isn't it? I've found references in old court documents, testimony from a trial in 1929. A man was arrested for bootlegging and claimed he'd been using 'underground routes' to move his product. The charges were eventually dropped, but the testimony mentioned basements that opened into other basements."

"So there really was a network."

"Almost certainly. But I've never been able to prove it. The properties have changed hands so many times, and most of the basements have been renovated or filled in. Your friend's discovery might be the first physical evidence."

"We'd like to explore it properly," Bob said. "Document what's there. But we could use an expert."

Fran's eyes lit up. "You want me to come take a look?"

"If you're willing."

"Willing? I've been waiting my whole career for an opportunity like this." She was already reaching for her jacket. "When can we go?"

* * *

Dylan Turner met them at the door an hour later, practically bouncing with excitement when Judy introduced Fran.

"A real historian," he said, shaking her hand vigorously. "This is exactly what I was hoping for."

They descended into the basement, now somewhat tidier than on their first visit. Dylan had cleared a path to the tunnel entrance and set up a work light that illuminated the opening.

"My contractor took a look yesterday," Dylan said. "He says the construction is solid. No signs of collapse or water damage. Should be safe enough to walk through, just watch your head."

Fran approached the wall slowly. She ran her fingers along the bricks, examining the mortar joints, the color variations, the way the wall met the floor.

"1920s construction," she confirmed. "Maybe 1924 or '25. Someone did careful work here. This wasn't a rush job."

She produced a flashlight from her bag and stepped into

the tunnel itself. Judy followed, with Bob and Dylan close behind.

The passage was narrow and dark, the air cool and carrying that mineral smell of old stone and earth. But with Fran's flashlight sweeping methodically across the walls, new details emerged.

"Look at this." Fran stopped about fifteen feet in, directing her beam at a section of the wall. "Scratches."

Judy leaned closer. The marks were faint, almost invisible unless you knew to look for them. Lines etched into the brick, arranged in a pattern.

"Initials?" she guessed.

"Possibly." Fran pulled out her phone and took several photographs. "T.B. and L.D., if I'm reading them correctly. And below that, what looks like a date. 1925."

Judy pictured the photograph Gladys had shown them, the two men standing side by side. They'd stood in this very passage, carving their initials into the brick.

"They signed their work," Bob said quietly.

"Or marked their territory." Fran moved deeper into the tunnel. "This is incredible. I need to measure everything, document the construction techniques, get samples of the mortar for dating."

They continued deeper. Judy noticed alcoves carved into the walls at irregular intervals, shallow recesses about two feet wide and a foot deep.

"Storage niches," Fran said, shining her light into one of them. "See the wear marks on the bottom? Something heavy sat here. Crates, probably. Or cases."

She reached into the alcove and pulled out a handful of rotted fabric, brown and brittle with age.

"Burlap," she said, holding it up for them to see. "They used to wrap individual bottles in burlap sacks stuffed with straw. Kept them from clinking together when they moved them. The sound of glass on glass would have given them away."

Cases of liquor, Judy thought. Stacked and waiting in the dark.

The tunnel curved gently to the left, and the ceiling dropped low enough that Bob had to duck. Cobwebs hung in thick curtains, undisturbed for decades. The floor beneath their feet changed from packed earth to old brick, worn smooth in the center from years of foot traffic.

"Someone walked this route a lot," Dylan said, noticing the same thing.

"Hundreds of times, probably. Maybe thousands." Fran paused to photograph a section of wall where the mortar had crumbled, revealing the original construction beneath. "This wasn't a shortcut someone used once or twice. This was a working corridor."

They passed another set of initials scratched into the brick, these ones harder to read. An R, maybe, and something that could have been a W or an M.

The tunnel had to extend well beyond Dylan's property line by now. Judy counted her steps. Forty. Fifty. Sixty.

Bob's foot kicked something that skittered across the brick floor. He bent down and picked it up.

"Cork," he said, holding it in his palm. It was darkened with age, compressed on one end where it had been pressed into a bottle neck. "Still in one piece."

Fran took it from him. "Whiskey bottle, probably. You can tell by the size." She handed it back. "Someone dropped this a hundred years ago. And here we are, picking it up."

The passage ended.

A wall of brick blocked their path. Unlike the passage walls, this barrier was rougher, the bricks mismatched, the mortar uneven.

"This was added later," Fran said, examining it closely.

"Different materials, different technique. Someone sealed this up."

"Where do you think it goes?" Dylan asked.

Fran checked something on her phone. "Based on the direction and distance, this wall should be right about at the property line. On the other side would be the neighboring basement."

"The yellow Victorian," Judy said.

"If I had to guess, I'd say this passage originally connected the two basements. At some point, someone bricked it up. Maybe when one of the properties changed hands, or when Prohibition ended and the tunnel was no longer needed."

"Can we open it?" Dylan asked.

Fran shook her head. "Not without permission from the neighboring property owner. And even then, we'd need to be careful. There's no telling what's on the other side. Could be another tunnel, could be a filled-in basement, could be nothing but dirt."

They spent another hour in the passage, Fran measuring distances and angles, photographing every detail, taking notes in a small leather journal. When they finally emerged into the basement, the afternoon light felt strange.

"So what's the next step?" Dylan asked.

"We need to talk to the neighbors," Fran said. "Convince them to let us look in their basement."

"The Harrisons," Dylan said. "They moved in a few months ago. I've waved but haven't really talked to them."

"You two might have better luck with the approach than me," Fran said. "People get suspicious when historians come knocking. They think we're trying to get their house declared a landmark or something."

Judy nodded.

"There's something else." Fran pulled the photos back out and pointed to a detail Judy hadn't noticed. A small symbol scratched into the brick near the initials. It looked like a light-house, crudely rendered but unmistakable. "I've seen this mark before. In documents from the period. It was a kind of signal, a way of marking safe routes or friendly properties. Houses that displayed this symbol were part of the network."

"So if we find this mark on other properties..." Bob began.

"Then we might be able to trace the entire system." Fran was practically vibrating. "This isn't just one tunnel. This is the first thread in something much bigger."

They said their goodbyes to Dylan and walked up the street toward the yellow Victorian. The house was quiet, no cars in the driveway, curtains drawn.

Bob rang the doorbell. They waited.

Nothing.

"Maybe they're at work," Judy said.

"Or on vacation."

They rang again, then knocked for good measure. Still nothing.

"We'll have to come back," Bob said.

Judy stood on the porch of the yellow house, wondering what secrets lay beneath it. Somewhere in that basement, if Fran was right, was the continuation of the passage they'd explored.

* * *

Lisa had been looking forward to clamming all day. She and Nick had gone out with Carol and Dennis a couple days ago for the first time, and she'd loved everything about it.

But when she walked out onto the deck, the stretch of shoreline where Carol and Dennis worked was empty. No Carol, no Dennis, no Roy.

Nick joined her at the railing. "Where is everyone?"

"I don't know." Lisa scanned the water. Nothing. "Maybe they're coming later?"

They waited fifteen minutes, watching the empty bay. A few boats moved in the distance, but no one appeared.

"I don't think they're coming," Nick said finally. "Could be anything—family stuff, doctor's appointment, who knows."

Lisa's shoulders sagged.

"We could go out ourselves," Nick said. "We've got the gear. Carol showed us the basics."

Lisa hesitated. They'd only been out once, and Carol and Dennis had done most of the guiding. Going alone felt risky.

"How hard can it be?" Nick spread his hands. "We know what to do."

The bay looked calm, and the afternoon felt too good to let pass.

"Okay," she said. "Let's try it."

They grabbed their rakes and mesh bags and walked down to the shore, stepping into the shallows without Carol and Dennis to follow.

They started in the spot where Carol had taken them, and found a few clams, but the pickings were thin. After twenty minutes, Nick straightened up and pointed north along the bay.

"What about over there? Past that little point. I noticed Carol glancing that direction when we were out with her."

Lisa wasn't sure. They'd never gone that far. "She kept us closer to shore."

"Maybe she's saving the good spots for herself." Nick grinned. "Come on. Let's explore a little."

They waded past the point Nick had indicated. The water was different here—a little deeper, the bottom firmer. Lisa dragged her rake through the sand and immediately felt resistance. She pulled up three clams in one stroke.

"This is more like it," she said.

They worked their way farther out, following the clams. The water crept up from knee-deep to thigh-deep, but neither of them paid much attention.

"Why didn't Carol bring us over here?" Nick said, dropping a handful into his bag. "This is way better."

Lisa laughed, but the pull against her legs had changed. Stronger. She looked back toward shore and felt her stomach drop.

They'd come much farther out than she'd realized. The bay house looked small in the distance. And the water that had been thigh-deep when they started was now up to her waist.

"Nick. The tide."

He looked around, his expression shifting. "When did that happen?"

"We need to head back."

They turned and started back. The current pushed against them, subtle but insistent. Each step took more effort than it should have. Lisa's feet sank into the soft bottom, and she had to pull them free with every stride.

"This is harder than I thought," Nick said. He was breathing heavier now, fighting the same resistance.

They'd made it maybe twenty yards when Lisa felt a nudge against her calf.

She froze. "Something touched me."

"Probably seaweed."

"It wasn't seaweed."

Then she saw it. A dark shape drifting below the surface, maybe two feet down. Broad and flat, with wing-like fins that flexed as it moved. Then another. And another.

"Nick. Look."

He followed her gaze down into the water. "What the—"

The rays were everywhere. Dozens of them, moving through the water in a slow, undulating mass. Cownose rays—she'd read about them somewhere, how they migrated through the bay in summer. Their wingspans were enormous, two or three feet across, and they moved with an eerie grace, wings rippling like birds in slow motion.

"Oh wow," Lisa breathed. "There's so many."

They kept coming. Wave after wave, gliding past like a scene from a nature documentary. One passed directly between her and Nick, close enough that she could have touched its smooth back. Another swept against her leg—not a sting, just the gentle pressure of a wing passing by. The water around them had become a river of wings, flowing steadily toward open water.

It was beautiful. It was also a problem.

"We can't walk through this," Nick said. "I can't even see the bottom."

He was right. The rays had turned the water into a shifting maze of shadows. Walking risked colliding with one, startling them, creating chaos.

So they stopped, watching for a gap. But the tide kept rising.

The water rose from Lisa's waist to her ribs. She watched the rays flow past, their movements hypnotic, and tried not to think about how much higher the water could go. The current tugged at her legs, stronger now. If she lost her footing, she'd be swept into the middle of the school.

"We need to start moving," she said.

They tried. But every step meant planting a foot blind into the thick of the rays, and the current fought them for every inch. After five minutes of effort, Lisa looked back and realized they'd barely covered ten yards. The water had reached her chest. She had to hold her rake above the surface, her arms starting to ache. The rays showed no sign of thinning.

"Lisa." Nick's voice had changed. "The water's still coming up."

"I know."

"If it gets much higher—"

"I know."

She glanced toward shore. It seemed impossibly far away.

Even if the rays cleared right now, they'd be fighting the current the whole way back, exhausted, in water up to their necks.

"We have to move faster," she said. "Rays or no rays."

Nick nodded. "Together. Don't rush."

They picked up the pace, placing each foot as carefully as speed allowed. The rays parted around them, unbothered, continuing their migration as if Lisa and Nick were just two more obstacles in the water. A wing grazed Lisa's hip. Another slid past Nick's thigh. But the rays didn't startle, didn't scatter— they just kept flowing, indifferent to the two humans pushing through their ranks.

The water was at Lisa's shoulders now. She had to tilt her chin up to keep her mouth clear. The current dragged at her with each stride, her legs burning from the effort.

Nick stumbled, caught himself, but his mesh bag slipped from his grip. "My clams—"

"Leave it." Lisa grabbed his arm.

"Almost there," Nick said. "Keep going."

The rays began to thin. The gaps between them grew wider. Lisa could see the sandy bottom again, could feel the water level starting to drop as they pushed into shallower territory.

Waist-deep. Then thighs. Then knees.

They made it onto the beach and dropped onto the sand, breathing hard. Lisa lay on her back, staring up at the sky, her heart pounding. Her whole body was shaking—not from cold, but from the adrenaline finally releasing.

"That was incredible," Nick said between breaths. "And terrifying. But mostly incredible."

Lisa turned her head to look at him. He was soaked, sandy, grinning like an idiot. She started laughing.

"We almost drowned watching fish," she said.

"Rays. Technically rays are—"

"I don't care what they technically are."

They were both laughing now, the relief making them giddy. Then Nick's face sobered. "That was close, though. Really close."

They sat there for a long moment, catching their breath, watching the water that had nearly swallowed them. Out where they'd been, Lisa could still see dark shapes moving beneath the surface—the tail end of the migration, continuing on as if nothing had happened.

"We got cocky," she said.

"We got stupid." Nick ran a hand through his wet hair. "There's probably a reason Carol didn't bring us out this far."

A voice called out from down the beach. "Lisa? Nick?"

Lisa looked up. Carol and Dennis were walking toward them along the water's edge, Roy a few steps behind. Their faces went from greeting to concern as they got closer.

Carol got a good look at them—soaked to their shoulders, pale, looking like survivors of a shipwreck. "What on earth happened?"

"We went out past the point," Lisa said. "The tide came in faster than we expected."

"We got caught in a ray migration," Nick added. "Couldn't tell where to step. Had to force our way out."

Carol and Dennis exchanged a look.

"The cownose fever," Dennis said. "They've been coming through all week. Hundreds of them." He looked out at the water then back at them. "You were stuck out there during that? While the tide was coming in?"

Nick nodded. "We didn't have much choice."

Carol sat down beside Lisa. "That spot past the point—the bottom drops off, and when the tide turns, it comes in fast. People have gotten into real trouble out there."

"The rays are harmless," she added. "Beautiful, actually. But you can't fight a migration like that, and if you're in the wrong place when the tide's moving..." She shook her head.

The reality of it was sinking in.

"We should have waited for you," she said.

"Yes." Carol didn't soften it. "You should have." Then her expression eased. "But you're okay. That's what matters. Now you know."

Dennis offered Nick a hand and pulled him to his feet. "You get any clams, at least? Before the excitement?"

Nick managed a weak laugh. "About a dozen. Dropped my bag somewhere back there when things got intense."

"I've still got mine." Lisa held up her mesh bag, still clipped to her belt. She'd forgotten she was even wearing it.

Carol smiled. "Then the afternoon wasn't a total loss. Come on—we were just checking the tide. Won't be right for clamming for a couple hours yet. Let's head back."

Lisa looked at Nick.

He shrugged. "I think I've had enough bay for one day."

They walked back to the house, Carol and Dennis and Roy falling into step beside them. Lisa's legs felt weak, her clothes were dripping, and she was pretty sure she'd be seeing those wings gliding through her dreams tonight.

Inside, Nick grabbed towels from the bathroom while Lisa peeled off her wet clothes.

"Shower's yours first," Nick said, handing her a towel. "You earned it."

"We both earned it."

She paused at the bathroom door. "Hey. Thanks for staying calm out there. I don't know what I would have done if you'd panicked."

"I was panicking on the inside." He smiled. "But you seemed like you had it together, so I figured I should fake it."

"Same."

That got them both. It had been terrifying, but they'd gotten through it together.

After hot showers and dry clothes, Lisa made pasta with the few clams she'd managed to keep—not enough for a proper feast, but enough to feel like they hadn't come home empty-handed.

Later, while Nick dozed on the couch, Lisa found herself standing in front of her boxes. She'd kept finding excuses not to deal with them.

She didn't want to put things off anymore. These boxes weren't going to unpack themselves.

She knelt down and pulled open the first one. Books, mostly. A few photo albums. And at the bottom, wrapped in newspaper, a framed print she'd almost forgotten she owned— a vintage travel poster of Paris, all pastel rooftops and golden light. She'd bought it years ago at a flea market, back when she'd dreamed of going someday.

She unwrapped it and held it up. It was cheerful, a little kitschy, completely out of place with Nick's laid-back beach aesthetic. But she loved it.

Nick stirred on the couch. "What's that?"

"Something I forgot I had." She turned it so he could see. "Probably doesn't fit with your decor."

He studied it for a moment then looked at the wall above the bookcase, where a black-and-white photograph of the Cape May lighthouse hung.

"That lighthouse photo came with the house," he said. "Previous owner left it. I never liked it much." He got up, crossed to the wall, and lifted the frame off its nail. "There. Now you've got a spot."

Lisa stared at the empty space on the wall. "You don't have to—"

"I want to." He set the lighthouse photo aside and took the Paris print from her hands, holding it up against the wall. "What do you think?"

The soft colors popped against the neutral walls. It looked nothing like the rest of the room. It looked like her.

"I think it works," she said.

Nick hung it, stepped back, and nodded. "Place was getting too beachy anyway. Needed some culture."

Lisa leaned into him. "Thank you."

"Don't thank me yet. You've still got boxes to go." But he was smiling. "This is your home too. It should look like it."

Lisa looked at the remaining boxes. One print on a wall didn't erase the feeling of being a guest in someone else's house. But it was a start.

CHAPTER SEVEN

Liz found Victor before she heard him, which was a first.

He was standing at the mouth of the entryway, arms folded, head tilted, watching a family of four disappear through the curved fabric passageway toward the Prism Corridor's true entrance. His silver hair was pulled back in a low ponytail, and he wore a collarless silk tunic so white it looked like it had never been touched by human hands. Adrian stood a few paces behind, tapping something into his phone.

Victor didn't move until the family had fully vanished behind the dark curtain. Then he turned, saw Liz, and pressed both hands to his chest.

"There she is," he said, his voice carrying the reverence of a man greeting a saint. "The architect of my salvation."

"Good morning, Victor."

"Good?" He strode toward her in three long steps and took her hands in his, rings clicking against her knuckles. "It is a magnificent morning." He released her and tilted his face to the sky, eyes closed. "It is a morning of vindication. A morning of triumph." He opened his eyes and swept his arm at the antechamber. "Look at what you've done."

Liz looked. The approach corridor worked. The matte

black fabric panels blocked the surrounding lawn from view, just as she'd planned, and the pathway curved gently to the right, preventing visitors from seeing the corridor's entrance until they were almost upon it. Small fans recessed along the base kept the fabric stirring, a subtle movement that made the walls feel alive.

They stepped inside together. The change was immediate. The noise of the festival, the crew chatter, the food truck generators, all of it fell away as the panels closed around them. The light dimmed. The air cooled. The pathway was narrow enough that their shoulders nearly touched, and the curve ahead hid whatever came next. A few paces in front of them, a young couple had gone quiet, the woman reaching out to brush her fingertips along the wall as they walked. Liz felt herself slow, her breathing settle. Even knowing exactly how it was built, she couldn't resist it.

"Watch them," Victor murmured, nodding toward the couple. "They came in talking. Now look." The couple had drawn closer together, their voices gone, their pace halved. Victor's eyes were bright. "Every time. Without exception. By the time they reach the threshold, they're prepared. They're ready to receive the work."

Liz had noticed. The whole thing worked the way she'd intended: a moment of transition between the ordinary world and the experience ahead.

"And the flow," Victor continued. "Not a single person has entered from the wrong end since the entryway went up. Not one. Foot traffic through the correct entrance is up ninety-four percent. The remaining six percent came in backwards despite the signage, which tells you everything you need to know about public literacy."

They emerged into the Prism Corridor itself. Even having seen it multiple times, Liz felt that catch in her chest. The floor caught every color the glass threw down. With each step the space opened, colors deepening—blues warming to greens, then amber, then gold. By the time they reached the final chamber, where a column of gold light struck the center of the floor, Liz had forgotten she was on a hotel lawn. Two women stood in that column, faces lifted, eyes closed. One of them was crying.

Victor watched them, his whole body still for once.

They stood together for a long moment. Then Victor turned to her.

"You gave me back my work," he said. "I won't forget that."

"You built something worth saving."

"Yes, well." He straightened the cuff of his silk tunic. "That goes without saying." But the corner of his mouth twitched. "Now go." He waved her away with a regal flick of his wrist. "Go do whatever it is you do that makes impossible things happen. I have a corridor to supervise."

She left him there, standing in the golden light with his arms behind his back, eyes tracking every visitor who filed through.

Outside, the June sun was already warming the pavement. Liz checked her phone—three items done, eleven to go.

Next stop: the Physick Estate grounds. The Gyre was part of the festival's second wave, opening tonight.

She cut through the quieter residential blocks, past Victorian porches and hydrangea gardens.

The Physick Estate appeared on her right, set back from Washington Street. The grounds had been partially roped off for the festival, and Liz could see the installation rising from the south lawn as she approached.

The Gyre was a twenty-foot spiraling tower built from interlocking driftwood beams, wrapped in oxidized copper wire, and studded with hand-blown glass spheres the size of softballs. Each sphere contained a small LED element that, at night, would illuminate from within, turning the entire structure into a column of twisting light. In daylight, the piece had a skeletal beauty, all angles and weathered grain and the soft green patina of the copper glinting in the sun.

Its creators were exactly where Liz expected to find them: on the grass at the base of the tower, cross-legged, eating what appeared to be granola out of mason jars.

Paisley looked up first. She was somewhere in her late fifties, with hair woven into a braid that fell past her shoulder blades. Wildflowers were tucked through the braid, purple clover and tiny white daisies. Her feet were bare and grass-stained, her cotton smock spotted with paint that had been there so long it had become part of the fabric.

"You're the one who fixed the corridor," Paisley said. Not a question.

"Word travels fast."

"Victor told everyone. He told the barista at the coffee shop. He told a dog. Sit down. Have you eaten? Bo made his cashew thing."

Bodhi unfolded himself from the grass. He was lanky and loose-limbed, barefoot like Paisley, with hair gathered and tied with a leather bootlace and beaded necklaces that clinked when he moved. He offered Liz a mason jar.

"Cashew, date, cacao, and something I found growing near the fence." He smiled. "Probably mint."

"Probably?"

"Eighty percent sure."

Liz laughed. "I'll take my chances." She accepted the jar and tried a spoonful.

"Bo used to be a structural engineer," Paisley said. "Built bridges in Oregon for twenty years. Now he builds sculptures and makes cashew paste."

"Don't let her fool you," Bo said. "She has a masters in materials science from MIT. She just doesn't like wearing shoes."

"Shoes interfere with ground energy."

"She's been saying that since 1994."

She walked a slow circle around The Gyre. The craftsmanship was exceptional—each driftwood beam followed its own arc, the spheres clustered more densely toward the top where the spiral narrowed.

"The base anchoring," Liz said, crouching near the steel plates bolted to concrete footings. "You poured these yourself?"

"Four days ago. Eighteen inches deep, rebar-reinforced." Bo knelt beside her. "Sandy soil's tricky, but we widened the footings at the bottom. Should hold."

Liz was about to compliment the glass work when she heard Megan's voice behind her, high and breathless.

"Liz! Oh, thank goodness. I've been looking everywhere." Megan appeared around the corner of the estate building, her hair held up with a single pencil today, the other one apparently lost. She was carrying a clipboard, a phone, and a paper bag from the coffee shop, all of which seemed on the verge of escaping her grip. "There's a situation at one of the beach installations, and there's an electrical panel issue on Beach Avenue, and I need you to look at the vendor layout for tomorrow's—"

A sound stopped her. Stopped all of them.

It started as a groan, low and structural, the kind of sound that buildings make in old movies right before they come apart. Liz's head snapped toward The Gyre. One of the steel brackets at the base had shifted. Not much. Maybe an inch. But on a twenty-foot tower, an inch at the bottom translated to a foot at the top.

The tower leaned.

"Everyone back!" Bo shouted, already moving, his bare feet covering the ground fast. He grabbed Paisley's arm and pulled her clear of the roped perimeter.

Liz was moving too, her hand finding Megan's elbow and hauling her backward. The tower swayed, the spheres catching the light as they tilted, throwing flashes of color across the grass.

Then the second bracket gave.

The Gyre came down in sections, the spiral unwinding as it fell. Driftwood beams snapped and scattered. Copper wire sang as it tore free. The spheres hit the ground in a cascade of breaking sound, shattering into starbursts of colored fragments that skittered across the lawn. The top of the tower struck the edge of the roped barrier, snapping one of the stanchions, and the whole thing settled into a heap of wood and wire and broken glass that bore no resemblance to the sculpture it had been thirty seconds earlier.

Dust rose. Then silence.

"Everyone okay?" Liz said.

Nods all around. Bo stood still, staring at the wreckage.

Megan's clipboard clattered to the grass. "Oh no. Oh no, no, no." She was scrolling through her phone with shaking hands. "This opens tonight. This is supposed to open tonight. What do we—how do we—" She looked at Liz, then at the mess on the lawn, then back at Liz. "Can we fix it?"

Bo dropped to one knee at the edge of the rubble, examining the steel bracket that had failed. "The footing shifted. Sandy soil. We accounted for it, but not enough." He held up the bracket. A clean fracture ran through the weld.

"Can you rebuild it by tonight?" Megan's voice had climbed an octave.

"Most of the glass is gone," Paisley said. "And seven beams snapped."

Megan stared at the ruins. Then she straightened. "Okay. We get duct tape, prop it up with sandbags, rope it off wider. And Christmas lights instead of the glass. From a distance, who's going to know?"

Bo and Paisley exchanged a look.

"It could work," Megan pressed. "We just need—"

"Megan," Liz said. "That's not going to work."

"Duct tape can't bear a structural load," Bo said quietly. "It comes down again, and next time there might be people inside the barrier."

Color rose in Megan's cheeks. "So what do you suggest?"

Liz turned to Bo. "How much is salvageable?"

"Sixty percent of the driftwood. The copper wire. Most of the hardware."

"What if you went shorter? Wider? Used only the undamaged beams."

Bo picked up two good beams, held them at angles. Something shifted in his expression. "Lower center of gravity. That could work."

"The spheres that survived, cluster them near the top. The missing ones, leave the mounts empty." Liz knelt and sketched in the dirt. "Call it intentional. Call it 'what survives.'"

"What survives," Paisley repeated. "That's not bad."

Bo was already sorting wood. "We'd need a welder and a few hours for new footings. But yeah. We can make sundown."

Megan stood apart, arms crossed. When Liz caught her eye, she didn't look away, but she didn't soften either.

"Megan, can you let the estate office know? There's going to be welding on their lawn."

"Sure." Her voice was flat. She picked up her clipboard and walked toward the building without looking back.

Paisley appeared beside Liz. "You two have history?"

"We went to art school together, but hadn't seen each other in twenty years. She brought me onto this project."

"Ah." Paisley watched Megan disappear around the corner. "Hard to watch someone else solve your problem."

* * *

Margaret pulled the volunteer lanyard over her head and adjusted the laminated badge so it faced forward. The Luminous Festival logo caught the last of the evening light as she and Dave made their way down the promenade toward the night's assignment.

They weren't at the Tidal Lumina tonight. Craig had shuffled the volunteer schedule, and their new post was a quarter mile down the beach, near the foot of Stockton Place, where a different installation had been drawing steady crowds all week. The Bloom covered a wide stretch of beach between the dune line and the surf—no structures, no sculptures, just the sand itself transformed. Projectors hidden along the dunes cast a wash of blue-green light across the ground, and wherever people walked, brighter blooms flared beneath their feet and slowly faded, so the beach seemed to pulse with bioluminescence. The effect was simple and strange: a hundred people wandering a dark beach, each one trailing light.

Ruthie was already there, thermos in hand, parked in a beach chair near the edge of the installation. Hank sat beside her, squinting at his phone like a man who refused to increase his font size.

"Glad you two signed up for this one," Ruthie said as Margaret and Dave settled into the other chairs. She unscrewed the thermos and poured into a plastic cup, shielding it with her body out of habit. "The Tidal Lumina's fine, but I needed a change of scenery. Same lights every night, you start dreaming in turquoise."

"She really does," Hank said without looking up. "Wakes me up talking about color temperatures."

"That happened once."

Hank held up three fingers without lifting his eyes from the phone.

Ruthie looked at Margaret. "He's keeping a log now. Like I'm a weather event."

Margaret accepted a cup and took a sip. Fruitier than the last batch.

"If Craig comes by," Ruthie said, "it's chamomile tea."

"Nobody drinks chamomile tea on a beach," Hank said.

Ruthie was already pouring.

Harper and Abby were back at the house with her parents, who'd offered to take them for pizza and a movie, which meant Margaret and Dave had the evening to themselves again.

The night eased in around them. Children ran through the lit sand, drawing bright patterns with their footsteps that lingered and faded. A couple slow-danced near the waterline, the glow pooling around them as they moved. The sky deepened from dusky blue to indigo, stars appearing one by one, and the projections intensified until the whole beach shimmered.

Around nine-thirty, Hank lowered his phone and sat up straighter.

"Look east," he said.

Margaret turned. At first she saw nothing unusual, just the flat line where the dark ocean met the darker sky. Then she noticed it. Low on the horizon, barely visible, a band of amber light spread across the water like a stain. It grew as she watched, intensifying from amber to deep orange, pushing upward against the night.

"Here it comes," Ruthie said.

The moon rose.

It came up slowly. Enormous. Impossibly large, the way the moon sometimes appeared when it was closest to the horizon, swollen and heavy and so vivid that Margaret's first instinct was that something was wrong with her eyes. The color was extraordinary: a deep, saturated orange that darkened to burnt umber at the edges, the craters and dark plains visible as shadowed topography across its face.

She'd known the moon would be close tonight—had read an article that morning about its orbit bringing it nearer to Earth this week. But no article had prepared her for this.

The moon cleared the horizon and hung above the water, its reflection stretching across the surface in a long copper smear. The moonlight hit the beach and the installation simply disappeared beneath it. The projected blue-green couldn't compete—the sand went amber, then white, the whole beach swallowed by something older and bigger than anything the festival could build. It didn't interact with the art. It replaced it.

The crowd had gone still. Even the children stood motionless. Margaret heard someone behind her whisper a word lost to the breeze, and then nothing, just the sound of the waves and the stillness of everyone watching. Dave leaned closer, his shoulder warm against hers.

"Now that's a moon," Hank said, his voice hushed.

"It's like it's right there," Ruthie said. "Like you could swim out and touch it."

Margaret was still watching, the moonlight bright on everything, when the shouting started.

It came from the far end of the beach. A man's voice, loud and sharp, cutting through the quiet.

"I'm not doing this anymore, Rachel! I told you three months ago, and you didn't listen, and I'm done pretending everything's fine!"

A woman's voice answered, lower but audible, strained with the effort of keeping herself together. "Can you please not do this here? People are staring."

"Let them stare! Maybe if somebody else hears this, you'll finally get that I'm serious!"

Margaret saw them now. A couple in their thirties, standing at the edge of the lit sand. The man was tall, with close-cropped hair and a polo shirt, his posture rigid with frustration. The woman was shorter, dark-haired, her arms wrapped around herself as if she were cold. The glow from the projections caught them from below, washing their faces in pale light, every gesture visible to the fifty people spread across the beach around them.

The mood shattered. Parents exchanged glances and began steering their children away. A teenage couple who'd been taking photos of the moon lowered their phones and edged toward the dunes. An older man in a fishing hat shook his head and moved on.

"Here we go," Hank muttered.

"This is supposed to be a vacation!" the woman said, her composure cracking. "You couldn't wait until we got back to the room?"

"A vacation? You think this is a vacation? You've been on your phone with your mother for three hours every day since we got here. Three hours! And then you act surprised when I'm in a bad mood."

"Don't bring my mother into this."

"Your mother is already in this! She's been in this since day one! She's more involved in our marriage than I am!"

The woman's voice broke. "That's not fair."

Margaret looked at Dave. His expression was the same one she was feeling: discomfort, annoyance, and the awkwardness of witnessing something deeply private in a public space. Around them, the remaining visitors shifted and murmured. The beautiful spell of the moonrise was gone.

Ruthie set down her cup. "Somebody needs to do something."

"Like what?" Hank said. "We're beach installation volunteers, not marriage counselors."

"They're ruining it for everyone."

"I know, but—"

Dave stood up from his chair. "I'll talk to them."

Margaret watched as he walked toward the couple, his pace easy, his posture open.

She was too far away to hear what he said when he reached them. He stood a few feet away and spoke quietly. The man turned toward him, his face flushed, his jaw set. For a second Margaret thought he might redirect his anger at Dave. But whatever Dave said next seemed to reach him. The man's shoulders dropped an inch. He looked at the woman, then at the crowd, and his expression changed.

The man said something Margaret couldn't catch, then turned and headed down the dune line, away from the installation, his hands shoved in his pockets. After a moment, the woman followed, keeping ten feet of distance between them.

Dave dropped back into his chair. "Suggested they might want some privacy. He agreed."

"What'd you say to him?" Ruthie asked.

"Told him there were fifty people out here who came to see something beautiful, and that whatever he was going through, it deserved a conversation, not an audience."

Ruthie raised her eyebrows. "And he just listened?"

"Nobody wants to be that guy. He just needed someone to remind him he was being that guy."

Ruthie nudged Hank. "We need Dave on every shift."

"Great," Hank said. "Then we'll be ready for the next marriage that falls apart at a light show."

The crowd began to settle. A few families who'd drifted away returned to their spots on the sand. The moonlight still poured down, steady and clear. The projections had come back faintly, blue-green light pooling in the spaces between people's shadows, but it felt like an afterthought now.

Twenty minutes later, Margaret was making her rounds when she spotted the woman. She was up on the lifeguard stand—the tall wooden one that had been dragged near the dunes for the night—sitting up in the seat with her knees pulled to her chest. The man was nowhere in sight.

Margaret hesitated. It wasn't her place. But the woman was sitting alone in the dark, and the beach was emptying out.

She walked to the base of the stand and looked up. "You okay?"

She looked down. Her eyes were dry, but her face carried exhaustion.

"Fine," she said. Then, after a pause: "Not fine. But you don't need to hear about it."

"I don't mind." She paused. "I'm Margaret."

The woman studied her for a moment. "He's not always like that. He's actually—" She stopped herself. Shook her head. "Everyone says that, don't they? 'He's not always like that.' Like it's an excuse."

"It's not an excuse. But it can still be true."

She was quiet. The waves rolled in, retreated, rolled in again.

"We were supposed to come here to fix things," the woman said finally. "New place, no distractions. Just us." She pulled at a thread on the hem of her shorts. "Turns out there's no beach pretty enough to fix what's actually broken."

Margaret climbed up and sat beside her.

"Rachel," the woman said.

They stayed like that for a few minutes, not speaking, watching the water. The moonlight lay across the ocean in a wide pale band, and the faint glow of the installation pulsed below them on the sand.

Eventually Rachel unfolded herself, climbed down, and looked back at Margaret with an expression that was hard to read.

"Funny thing is," she said, "things feel clearer right now than they have in months." She gave a half laugh, tired but real. "Guess that's something."

She turned and walked up the beach toward the street, her silhouette fading against the glow of the streetlights until she disappeared around the corner of a beach house.

Margaret made her way down and crossed the sand back to the chairs. Dave looked up as she took the seat beside him.

"Everything okay?"

"The woman from earlier," Margaret said. "She was up on the lifeguard stand by herself. I kept her company for a bit."

Dave nodded. He didn't ask what they talked about.

Ruthie poured her a fresh cup from the thermos. Light drifted across the sand, a few last visitors wandering through, their footsteps blooming and dimming.

CHAPTER EIGHT

Donna had been on Higbee Beach for nearly an hour, and she'd found two small shark teeth. The tide was cooperating, pulling back slow and steady, exposing fresh gravel in long dark bands along the waterline. Clyde had told her to watch for mornings like this, when the conditions lined up just right and the beach gave up its secrets without a fight.

They'd set up near a flat rock at the top of the tide line—a shared bucket, towels, water bottles. Dale was working a strip of dark sediment twenty yards to her left, crouched at the waterline with his sifting screen, shaking handfuls of sand and letting the finer material fall through. She watched him pause, hold something up to the pale light, and drop it into his bag. Three outings in, and he'd developed an eye for it. He could tell a tooth from a pebble at arm's length.

The fog had come in again overnight, though not as thick as their last visit. Donna could see maybe forty feet in every direction, enough to make out a couple working near the dunes and a man with a bucket farther south. Clyde was thirty yards north, moving at his usual unhurried pace.

Donna knelt in the gravel. It was denser here than usual, a good patch exposed by the retreating tide, and she sifted through it with her fingers. A shard of shell. A worn black pebble. Another pebble. Then something with an edge to it, a curve that didn't belong to erosion.

The tooth was nearly an inch long, dark gray, slender and slightly curved with smooth cutting edges. The root was intact, fanning out at the base. She knew this shape from the identification charts she'd been studying. Mako. And a good one.

She turned it over. Eight million years, maybe more, sitting in the dark while the world rearranged itself overhead.

"Dale." She held it up. "Look at this."

He crossed the distance and leaned in for a closer look. "That's your best one yet."

"Mako."

She carried it back to the bucket and set it inside, nestled among the smaller teeth, a few pieces of sea glass, and a cloudy quartz pebble Dale had found earlier. Then she returned to her spot and kept working. This was the part she loved—no agenda, no schedule, just scanning and sifting while the ocean did its work a few feet away.

It was Clyde who interrupted.

He appeared beside them without his usual greeting, his eyes fixed on something down the beach. "You two need to see this."

Donna stood and followed his gaze south. Through the thinning fog, maybe a hundred yards away, a group of people had gathered near the water's edge. Six or seven of them, clustered together, moving along the beach in a slow pack. She could hear their voices carrying across the sand. Excited. Loud. People who thought they were getting lucky.

And at the front of the group, leading them like a guide, was Garret.

"Since when does he bring people out here?" Donna asked.

"That's what I'd like to know." Clyde's voice was level. "He's always been a solo operator. Every time I've seen him on this beach, he's been alone with his screen and his bucket. And he's not the type to share his spots. This is new."

They watched. Even from this distance, Donna could see the tourists were finding things. Constantly. A woman in a pink visor raised something and squealed. A man bent to sift for maybe thirty seconds, then stood with his fist in the air. Two teenagers hunched over the same spot, pulling teeth out of the sand like they were picking berries.

"Nobody finds that many teeth that fast," Donna said. "Not even on a good day."

"No," Clyde said. "They don't."

Dale had been watching too. "Maybe it's just a hot spot. We've hit good patches before."

"You've hit patches where you find a tooth every ten or fifteen minutes if you're lucky," Clyde said. "Those people are finding something every thirty seconds. Watch the pattern. They're not even searching. They're just reaching down and picking things up."

He was right.

"He salted it," Donna said.

Clyde nodded slowly. "Before they got here. Probably walked that section at first light and scattered teeth through the gravel. High-quality stuff, big enough to spot without a screen. Then he brings in his group and lets them go."

"But why?" Dale asked. "He'd be giving away inventory."

"Unless the inventory isn't real." Clyde started walking south, not toward the group but at an angle, cutting inland toward a stretch of beach the tour had already passed through. Donna and Dale followed. The fog still hung thick enough here to screen them from view.

Clyde stopped where the group had started their walk, a swath of churned-up sand near a cluster of rocks. He dropped to his knees and began sifting through it, his fingers quick and sure.

After a minute, he lifted a tooth.

About an inch and a half long, dark brown, with a polished sheen that caught the light. Donna could see the difference immediately. Every tooth she'd ever pulled from this beach had imperfections. Chips, mineral deposits, irregular coloring, rough patches where the enamel had worn in unpredictable ways. This one was uniform. Smooth. Almost glossy.

Clyde held it up to the light. "This isn't from here."

"How can you tell?" Dale asked.

"Color's wrong for Delaware Bay sediment. The teeth we find here absorb iron and manganese from the local geology. They come out brown, sometimes reddish, sometimes gray or black. This is a flat chocolate color with no variation at all." He held it closer. "And feel the surface. It's been tumbled. Probably in a rock polisher with some kind of abrasive. Then oiled to bring out the color."

Donna took it from him. The surface had an unnatural slickness, nothing like the rough, mineral-crusted texture of the teeth in her bag.

"You can buy teeth like this in bulk online," Clyde said. "Moroccan, mostly. Indonesian. A hundred of them for fifty dollars. Clean them up, polish them, scatter them on a beach." He looked toward the tour group, still working their way south, their laughter audible even at this distance. "Then charge people a hundred and fifty a head for a 'premium guided fossil hunting experience.' Everyone goes home happy with a bag full of teeth they think they pulled from ancient New Jersey seafloor."

"And the real teeth?" Donna asked.

"Meanwhile, whatever he finds on his own—the real local teeth—those end up on his website. 'Authentic Delaware Bay fossils.' He gets to keep his actual inventory while charging tourists for fakes."

Dale watched the tour group recede into the fog. Garret

was pointing at something in the sand, his tourists gathered around him. Playing the expert. "So the whole tour is a con."

"There's more," Clyde said. "I've had finds go missing on this beach. Other collectors have too. Bags left unattended for a few minutes. Buckets that disappear. Always on days when Garret's out here. Always when the fog's thick enough to cover someone's tracks."

By the time Clyde finished, the stretch of beach where the tour had been was empty.

Donna looked back toward where she and Dale had been working. Their bucket sat on the sand near the rock, visible but distant. She hadn't been watching it.

"Let's head back," she said.

They walked quickly. The fog was thinning now, the June sun starting to burn through, and their section of beach came into view. The rock. The spot where they'd left their bucket.

The bucket was gone.

She stopped walking. Stared at the empty sand where a morning's work had been sitting fifteen minutes ago.

"Dale."

He saw it at the same moment. His face went blank, then red.

"It was right there," he said. "Right next to the rock."

"I know."

Clyde didn't say anything. He walked to the spot, knelt, and studied the sand like it was evidence. Then he straightened and looked toward the parking lot.

"Stay here."

He was gone for five minutes. When he came back, he shook his head.

"His truck's gone. Tour must have wrapped up while we were talking."

Dale's hands had curled into fists at his sides. "I had three teeth in there. My best day yet."

"I know," Clyde said.

"And Donna's mako."

The three of them stood there while the beach revealed itself as the fog lifted. Other hunters were arriving now, fresh faces with fresh bags, spreading out along the shore with no idea what had just happened.

"I can't prove he took them," Donna said.

"No." Clyde reached into his vest and pulled out the polished tooth he'd picked up from Garret's tour route. "But this is something. And it's not the first one I've found. I've been picking these up at his spots for months. Different beaches, same product. Same polished finish and bulk coloring." He tilted it toward the light. "I've been photographing them. Logging the dates and locations. I just didn't have enough to know what it meant."

"And now you do," Dale said.

"Now I do. He's running paid tours on public beaches with planted material. That's fraud. And if he's taking other people's finds on top of it, that's theft." Clyde pocketed the tooth. "I know a ranger with Fish and Wildlife who's been curious about the volume Garret moves online. He's never had a reason to look into it. This might be one."

Donna looked at the empty sand where their bucket had been. The mako tooth. A minute in her hand, and now it was probably rolling around in the bed of a black pickup heading north.

But the beach would keep giving. The tides didn't stop. Every low tide laid out something new for whoever had the patience to look. She'd find another mako. A better one, maybe.

* * *

Sarah drove the length of Dorothy's street twice before finding a spot three blocks away. She stopped counting cars at twenty.

They lined both sides of the road as far as she could see,

parked bumper to bumper, some angled onto the grass where the curb disappeared. A minivan was attempting a three-point turn near the corner, blocking a sedan trying to get past. Two women she didn't recognize walked briskly up the sidewalk carrying folding chairs, consulting their phones.

She sat in the car. The first Books by Moonlight had drawn maybe thirty people, most of them regulars from the shop. That was three days ago—the first of three events she'd pitched to Dorothy. She'd sent this one to the Book Nook email list—sixty-three subscribers. Twenty had RSVP'd. Apparently they'd brought friends.

Books by Moonlight was supposed to be simple—bring a chair or a blanket, listen to an author read, talk about books with neighbors under the stars.

After the first event, Sarah had called Dorothy. No harpist this time, she'd said. No photographer, no velvet ropes, no rows of organized chairs, no aspic molds. Just books and a garden and whatever food Dorothy wanted to make. Dorothy had been quiet on the other end before agreeing—a silence Sarah suspected cost her something.

Dorothy was on the front porch, and for the first time since Sarah had known her, she looked rattled.

"How many people did you invite?" Dorothy asked as Sarah came up the walk.

"I sent it to the email list. Sixty-three people. Twenty RSVP'd."

"Then explain this." Dorothy gestured at the street. "They haven't stopped coming for the last ten minutes."

The garden was beautiful, but it was a garden. Winding paths and delicate plantings and decades of roses that had taken a lifetime to cultivate. Not a venue. Not a park.

The garden filled fast. Blankets appeared between flower beds. Camp chairs blocked the flagstone paths. A woman in wedge sandals stepped directly into a bed of lavender to angle her phone for a photo. A child was already throwing pebbles at the koi.

"If anyone touches Walter's roses," Dorothy murmured, "I will lose my composure entirely."

By seven-thirty, at least sixty people had packed themselves into a space designed for garden parties of thirty. Sarah was hauling a second cooler from her car when she spotted the author.

Norman Quick was local the way a barnacle is local. Three self-published detective novels and an author photo that showed a serious man in a crisp blazer with a carefully maintained combover. The man approaching her wore the blazer, wrinkled, and the combover had lost its battle with the humidity. He carried a glass of something amber that was definitely not iced tea.

"Sarah!" He bypassed her extended hand and pulled her into a hug that lasted three seconds too long and smelled like bourbon. "What a turnout. And this garden. Like something out of a magazine. A little crowded, maybe. But the bones are good."

He headed straight for the refreshment table, where Dorothy had abandoned the aspic molds and crudité tree from last time in favor of bruschetta and caprese skewers.

"Bruschetta," Norman said, picking one up and examining it the way a jeweler might inspect a suspect stone. "Needs more basil. The bread should be crunchier." He ate it in one bite. "Tomatoes aren't local yet." He shook his head. "You can taste it."

He refilled his glass from a bottle he'd apparently brought in his blazer pocket. "So where's the green room?"

"There's no green room. It's a garden."

"Right, right. Quaint. I did a reading at a vineyard in Napa once. They had a green room. And a sound system. And a cheese board that would make you weep." He took a long sip. "But this works too."

Dorothy appeared beside Sarah the moment Norman wandered off. "Where did you find this person?"

"He contacted me. His books had decent reviews."

"He's been drinking."

"I noticed."

"I heard him criticize my bruschetta."

Dorothy's expression could have frozen the Delaware Bay.

What followed was an exercise in containment. Norman worked the crowd like a politician at a fundraiser, telling everyone about his novels, his screenplay in development with "a very interested producer in Burbank," and a fishing trip involving a man named Paulie who was possibly connected to organized crime in Atlantic City. He complimented women on their outfits in ways that made them step backward. He found the lemon tart, ate two slices, and announced to the people nearby that it was "a solid seven out of ten."

Sarah was putting out fires. Literally, in one case, when a citronella candle tipped over near the pergola and singed a patch of ivy. She stomped it out and turned around to find a line of people at her book table, most of them asking not for books but for directions to the bathroom.

"There's one inside the house," she said for the fifth time. "Through the back door, first on the left."

She found Dorothy in the kitchen managing the bathroom queue with the efficiency of a nightclub bouncer. Seven people stretched through the sunroom, past Walter's reading chair, into the hallway.

"This is unsustainable," Dorothy said. "One bathroom. One. Someone left a wine glass on Walter's end table. Someone else asked if the china cabinet was for sale."

Back in the garden, a woman had gotten tangled in the climbing roses near the back fence while trying to photograph them, her sleeve snagged on thorns, three blooms snapped from their stems and lying on the ground.

Dorothy came outside just as Sarah reached her. She saw the fallen roses and stopped.

"Those are the Graham Thomas climbers," she said quietly. "Walter grafted them himself."

Then she was moving, hostess smile gone. She freed the woman from the thorns with terrifying grace, collected the broken blooms, and said something too low for Sarah to hear. The woman left the garden within two minutes.

Sarah saw her hurry toward the gate. Then she climbed the gazebo steps and raised her voice.

"Everyone—can I have your attention?" The crowd quieted, faces turning toward her. "We're thrilled so many of you came tonight. But this garden is a private home, not a public park, and it's been entrusted to us. Please stay on the paths. Please don't touch the plantings. And please remember that the roses you're standing next to are forty years of some-one's life."

A few people shifted guiltily away from the flower beds. Others nodded. It wasn't a perfect fix, but the energy changed slightly—less like a free-for-all, more like guests who'd been reminded they were guests.

At eight o'clock, Norman took the microphone.

"I'm going to read from chapter fourteen tonight. It's about twenty pages. Thirty, if I do the voices."

He did the voices. The detective got a gravelly baritone. The marina owner got a nasal whine. A female witness got a breathy falsetto that made several women in the audience exchange uncomfortable looks. Norman paced the gazebo with the theatrical commitment of a man who believed himself to be performing Shakespeare at the Globe.

Ten minutes passed. Fifteen. Twenty. People fidgeted in their chairs. Whispers started. The teenagers near the koi pond returned to their phones.

At the twenty-five-minute mark, he paused for a drink and

launched into an eight-minute anecdote about the "real-life inspiration" for the scene. Then he kept reading. He did a voice for a seagull.

Dorothy stepped close. "This needs to stop."

"I agree. How?"

"Follow my lead."

She walked to the portable speaker, found the power cable, and pulled it.

Norman's amplified voice vanished. He tapped the dead microphone. Looked at Sarah.

"Technical difficulties," Dorothy said, stepping onto the gazebo with seamless composure. "We're going to take a brief intermission. Please help yourselves to refreshments." She turned to Norman and spoke quietly enough that only he and Sarah could hear. "That was lovely. We're transitioning to the social portion of the evening now."

"But I was just getting to the twist—"

"And what a twist it must be. You can tell people about it individually during the reception. They'll be lining up to ask." Her smile could have moved continents. "Trust me."

Norman looked at the crowd, already heading for the food table with visible relief. "You're good," he said.

"Thirty years of garden parties."

Sarah watched from the garden path. They'd both stepped in tonight—Sarah with the announcement, Dorothy with the power cable. And Dorothy hadn't steamrolled the way she had last time. She'd read the room.

Dorothy caught her eye across the garden and nodded. Not a victory lap. An acknowledgment. We did this.

The rest of the evening became what Sarah had originally envisioned. Without the microphone, the garden relaxed. People talked. They clustered along paths and on benches, discussing books and stories and what it meant to be sitting in this extraordinary space on a June evening with the scent of roses and the sound of crickets beginning in the hedgerow.

Norman, separated from his amplified platform, turned out to be tolerable in small doses. Several people bought his book. One woman told him the seagull voice was the highlight of her week, and Sarah couldn't tell if she was being sincere.

Sarah sold more books in the next hour than she had all week at the shop. People asked about the next event before this one ended. A man handed her a business card and said he owned a bookshop in Wildwood and wanted to try something similar.

Near the end of the night, she found Dorothy on the bench beside the koi pond, shoes off, feet tucked beneath her.

"I owe you an apology," Sarah said, sitting down. "For the first event. I should have told you sooner what I didn't want."

"I owe you one as well. I treated your event like mine." Dorothy paused. "Walter used to say I could commandeer a PTA meeting the way Sherman marched to the sea."

Sarah laughed. "That sounds about right."

"Tonight was different, though."

"Tonight I pulled the plug on a man doing a seagull impression in my garden." Dorothy looked at the trampled grass, the footprints in the flower beds, the broken roses she'd collected and placed in a vase on the refreshment table. "But for the first time in three years, this garden sounded the way it used to. Like a place where people actually gathered."

The koi moved in slow circles beneath the lily pads, unbothered by everything that had passed over their domain.

"We need a plan for next time," Sarah said. "A real plan. Guest limit, food budget, and a reading that doesn't exceed twenty minutes under any circumstances."

"Forty people maximum. RSVP only, no exceptions."

"And anyone who steps off the path gets one warning."

Dorothy smiled. "Books by Moonlight, volume three."

"Heaven help us."

Sarah gathered her things and walked to her car. The street was quiet now, the last visitors gone, the neighborhood returned to itself. She loaded the coolers into the trunk and paused, looking back toward Dorothy's house, where a single porch light burned against the dark.

The night had changed things. Not just between her and Dorothy, though that was part of it. Sarah had a plan now. And for the first time, she believed it might actually work.

CHAPTER NINE

The yellow Victorian stood bright in the morning sun, its cheerful paint the color Gladys had complained about. Shoulder to shoulder with Dylan Turner's house, the two looked like old friends who'd stopped speaking. Today, with Fran Martino beside her and Bob parking the car down the block, the house was finally ready for them.

A woman answered the door before Judy could knock. She was in her mid-thirties, with short dark hair and a dust mask pushed up on her forehead, a roller brush still in her hand.

"You must be the history people," she said. "I'm Carrie. Come on in. I've been dying to show someone what we found."

Judy looked at Fran, who raised her eyebrows. They'd called ahead to explain they were researching Prohibition-era construction, and mentioned the tunnel Dylan had discovered next door. Dylan had wanted to join them, but his contractor was finally available to fix the water damage that had started all this. The Harrisons' response had been immediate and enthusiastic.

"Darren's in the basement already," Carrie said, leading them past exposed framing and plastic sheeting. "He's been down there since breakfast. Fair warning, he gets excited."

The basement stairs were narrow and steep, the treads dipped in the center from decades of use. Judy descended with one hand on the rail and emerged into a room nothing like Dylan's cluttered renovation site. Everything had been cleared to the studs. Work lights hung from temporary hooks, illuminating every corner. Against the far wall, a man in his forties stood beside an opening in the foundation that hadn't been there a week ago.

"They're here!" He crossed the room and shook hands with each of them in turn, clasping with both of his. "I'm Darren. Darren Harrison. Carrie's husband. We bought this place last year. The tunnel's incredible. Absolutely incredible."

Fran had moved to the entrance, her flashlight playing across the darkness beyond. "When did you find this?"

"Four days ago. We were repointing the foundation—replacing the old mortar where it had crumbled—and Carrie noticed the bricks behind it were a different color. We pulled out three of them and—" He gestured at the hole. "There it was. Just sitting there behind the wall like it had been waiting for us."

The opening was roughly three feet wide and five feet tall, framed by the same style of brickwork Judy remembered from Dylan's tunnel. She stepped closer and peered inside. The passage extended into shadow, angling slightly to the left.

"Watch your heads," Carrie said from the stairs. "Darren's been down there a dozen times already, but I still get nervous."

Fran was already snapping photos of the frame, the transition between the original foundation stones and the newer brick. "This construction matches what we found next door. Same era, same technique. I'd bet money they were built at the same time, probably by the same crew."

Bob pulled out his phone and started documenting while Fran worked. Judy stepped into the tunnel, ducking slightly to clear the low ceiling. The air was different here, cooler and drier than the basement behind her, carrying the same mineral smell she'd noticed at Dylan's.

"There's more," Darren said. "Come look at this."

He led them along the passage, which curved before opening into a small chamber about eight feet square. The walls here were red brick as well, but built with even more care, the joints tight and uniform.

A brass tube, about two inches in diameter, protruded from the wall at eye level. It was tarnished green with age, but when Judy brushed her fingers across it, she could feel the smooth curve of a mouthpiece at one end.

"A speaking tube," Fran said. "I've read about these but never actually seen one in the field."

"What is it?" Carrie asked.

"Communication system. They ran brass tubes through the walls between properties so people could talk to each other without leaving their basements. During Prohibition, if one house got raided, they could warn the others." Fran traced the tube's path upward, where it disappeared into the brick. "This probably connects to Dylan's house next door. Maybe others too."

"We didn't see anything like this on Dylan's end," Judy said.

"Maybe it's behind the bricked-up wall," Bob said. "Or plastered over."

The basement's work lights didn't reach this far into the tunnel. Their flashlight beams made the chamber feel smaller, the shadows deeper where the light didn't touch.

Darren nodded. "We figured it was something like that. But that's not all. Look over here."

He crossed to the opposite wall and pointed to a section where the bricks had been laid at a slight angle, creating a slanted channel about a foot wide that ran from near the ceiling down to the floor.

"A chute," Judy said.

"For bottles, we think. Or crates." Darren ran his hand

along the smooth interior of the channel. "It opens into the floor of a closet upstairs—we thought it was just a weird patch job until we found this end. You could slide things down from one level to another. If someone was loading from upstairs, they could send cases down to the basement without carrying them. Or if they needed to move product between properties fast—"

"They could use the tunnel and the chute together," Fran finished. "Load here, slide down, move through the passage, load up on the other end." She was scribbling in her notebook. "This is sophisticated. This wasn't some amateur operation. A professional designed this system."

They spent another hour documenting everything. Fran measured the speaking tube's diameter and angle, traced the bottle chute's path. Bob took dozens of photos from every angle.

Judy was examining the chute more closely, shining her flashlight into its depths, when she noticed something wedged at the bottom where the channel met the floor. It was stuck in the corner, almost invisible in the shadows.

"Bob, look at this."

He joined her. She reached in and worked the object free— a tin box, about the size of a paperback book, its surface corroded but intact. The lid was stuck, sealed by decades of rust and grime.

"Someone hid this in the chute," Fran said, kneeling beside them. "Probably slid it down from upstairs and forgot about it. Or couldn't retrieve it." She turned it over carefully. "Whatever's inside could be fragile."

They carried it upstairs to the kitchen, where Carrie cleared the counter and produced a butter knife. Fran worked the lid with patience, easing it up millimeter by millimeter until it released with a soft pop.

Inside, wrapped in oilcloth that had somehow survived the years, was a thin bundle. Judy unfolded it and spread the contents on the counter.

Three photographs, their edges brown with age.

The first showed two men standing in front of what might have been a warehouse—Judy recognized Leon Dotson from Gladys's photograph. The second showed a group gathered around a long table, bottles visible, everyone raising glasses toward the camera. Among the faces, Judy spotted someone who might have been Gladys's grandfather.

The third photograph was different. A woman, young and pretty, posed alone on a dock. She wasn't smiling. Her expression was troubled, her arms crossed over her chest. On the back, in faded pencil: "Alice. 1926."

"We need to show this to Gladys," Judy said.

* * *

They phoned Gladys before driving over. She answered on the second ring and listened without interrupting as Judy described what they'd found. When Judy finished, the line went quiet.

"Come over," Gladys said. "Bring the photographs."

Gladys was waiting on the porch when they arrived. She looked smaller than she had during their first visit, her shoulders hunched slightly, her hands clasped in her lap. She didn't invite them inside. Instead, she gestured to the wicker chairs arranged around a low table.

"Show me," she said.

Judy laid the pictures out one by one. Gladys studied each without speaking. When she reached the picture of Alice, her hands trembled.

"That's Alice Dotson." Gladys's voice caught. "Leon's daughter."

Judy waited.

"I told you the Brocades and Dotsons were friends. Partners, even. What I didn't tell you was how it ended." Gladys picked up the picture of Alice and held it at arm's length,

117

squinting at the faded image. "Alice was engaged to my uncle. The wedding was supposed to unite the families, make the partnership permanent. But something happened in 1926. I don't know the details. My grandmother would never speak of it. All I know is the engagement was broken, Alice left for Philadelphia, and the two families never spoke again."

"The picture is dated 1926," Fran said. "Right when everything fell apart."

Gladys set it down. "My grandfather was not a perfect man. I told you he did what he had to do during hard times. But there were rumors even when I was a girl that he'd cheated someone. That he'd taken more than his share and let someone else bear the consequences."

"Leon's family?" Bob asked.

Gladys didn't answer directly, but her voice had hardened. "What I know is that after 1926, the silence between them was total. When my grandfather died in 1941, no one from the Dotson side came to the funeral. Whatever happened, it wasn't forgiven."

"Do you know what happened between them?" Judy asked. "What caused the break?"

Gladys was quiet for a moment. The sky had darkened while they talked, and rain began tapping on the porch roof.

"There were stories," she said finally. "My grandmother told them to me when she thought I was asleep. Stories about someone who got hurt. Someone who paid a price that others should have shared." She looked at Judy, and there was fear in her eyes, and resignation too. "I've spent my whole life protecting this family's name. But maybe some things shouldn't stay buried forever."

She stood, gathering the pictures. For a moment Judy thought she was going to send them away. But Gladys stayed where she was, gazing past them toward the street.

"My grandmother kept a letter," she said. "She hid it in her sewing box, and I found it after she died." She turned to face them. "I've never shown it to anyone."

"You don't have to—" Judy began.

"Yes, I do." Gladys's voice was steady now. "I've carried this long enough."

She went inside. They waited on the porch, not speaking, the steady drip from the eaves the only sound. When she returned, she carried a small envelope, yellowed and soft with age.

"In 1926, there was a raid," Gladys said. "Federal agents. Someone had tipped them off about a shipment coming through. Leon was in the tunnel when they came." She paused. "He was caught."

Judy felt Bob shift beside her.

"What happened to him?" Fran asked.

"He fell running in the dark. Hit his head on the brick. The agents found him unconscious." Gladys paused. "My grandfather was supposed to be there that night. He was the one who usually handled the deliveries on this end. But he wasn't there. He'd received a warning and stayed home."

"He didn't warn Leon," Bob said.

"No. He didn't." Gladys opened the envelope and unfolded the paper inside. "This is from Alice. She wrote it the week before her wedding was supposed to happen. She'd found out somehow—maybe she overheard something, maybe she just put the pieces together. But she knew."

She handed the letter to Judy. The handwriting was careful, deliberate. But the anger was unmistakable.

"I know what you did," Judy read aloud. "I know you let my father take the fall to save yourself. I won't marry into a family built on that kind of cowardice. Don't try to contact me. As far as I'm concerned, the Brocades are dead to us."

The rain drummed overhead. No one knew what to say.

"My grandfather kept this his whole life," Gladys said. "And my grandmother kept it after he died. And I've kept it since she passed. Three generations of silence." She took the letter back, folded it carefully, and slipped it into the envelope. "Leon never recovered. He died in 1932, broken and poor. He's buried in the Cold Spring cemetery. No marker—Alice couldn't afford one. I've thought about putting one up. Never had the courage."

Judy watched Gladys, still holding the envelope.

"Why tell us now?" she asked.

Gladys considered the question. "Because you found the pictures. Because Alice deserves to be more than a sad woman in a faded image. Because Leon deserves to be remembered." She met Judy's eyes. "And because I'm eighty-nine years old, and I'm tired of carrying it alone."

She pressed the envelope into Judy's hands.

"Take it," she said. "Write your history. Tell the truth. I'm done protecting ghosts."

They said their goodbyes and walked to the car through the rain. They were halfway down the block before anyone spoke.

"That's not what I was prepared for," Fran said quietly.

Bob shook his head. "It never is."

"There's still more," Fran said, and this time there was energy in her voice. "The speaking tubes, the network—those other houses were part of this too. We're just getting started."

Judy looked back at the house. Gladys was still on the porch, but she didn't look small anymore. She stood straighter than she had all afternoon, her shoulders back, watching them go. She raised one hand—not quite a wave, more like a release.

Then she turned and went inside, and for the first time in a long time, the house didn't look like it was keeping secrets.

* * *

Lisa heard voices drifting up from the bay.

She stepped onto the deck and listened. Laughter, the splash of water, a woman's voice calling words she couldn't make out. Nick had gone down an hour ago, leaving her to finish the book she'd been reading all afternoon.

The afternoon tide had come in perfectly. Carol and Dennis were visible at the waterline, along with Roy, all three of them waist-deep and working their rakes through the sand.

Nick was already in the water with them. He saw her on the deck and waved, gesturing for her to come down.

Lisa stretched, feeling the pleasant ache in her shoulders from yesterday's unpacking. She went inside to change, pulling on the old shorts and T-shirt she'd designated for clamming, then grabbed her gear and headed for the water.

The day was clear and still, the bay so calm it could have been glass. Lisa could see the bottom through the water, every ripple of sand, every shell and stone.

"There she is," Carol called. "We were starting to think you'd gone soft on us."

"Never." Lisa waded in, the water cold at first against her calves, then almost pleasant as her body adjusted. She positioned herself near Carol, finding her spot in the familiar formation they'd developed over the past week.

The work came easily now. Lisa knew where to look, how to read the subtle differences in the sand that signaled clams below. Her rake moved in smooth arcs, and she felt the telltale resistance on her first pull. Three clams.

"Not bad," Dennis said, watching her.

"She's got the touch," Roy added. It was the most words he'd strung together in Lisa's presence.

They worked in rhythm, the five of them spread across the shallows, rakes rising and falling in a pattern they no longer had to think about. Time slipped away, as it always did out here. Just the rake, the sand, the clams.

An hour passed. Maybe more. The sun dropped lower, the light turning golden across the water. Her bag was heavy against her hip, heavier than it had ever been.

"Check your count," Carol said.

Lisa unclipped her bag and counted. Forty-seven. The recreational limit was fifty.

"I'm at forty-two," Nick said from a few yards away.

Dennis whistled. "You two are going to hit your limit before we do."

Lisa had never hit the limit before. The first few times out, she'd been lucky to find a dozen. Then twenty. Then thirty. But fifty had always felt out of reach, the mark of experienced clammers, not newcomers still learning to read the bottom.

She slowed down, aware of each clam, counting as she went. Forty-eight. Forty-nine. And then fifty.

"That's it," she said. "I'm done."

Nick smiled. "Same. Fifty exactly."

Carol straightened up, hands on her hips, studying them both. Her expression was hard to read.

"Well," she said. "I guess you two don't need me anymore."

Nobody said anything. It was true, in a way. They knew what they were doing now. They could come out here alone, find the clams, hit their limit, go home satisfied. They didn't need Carol to guide them anymore.

But that wasn't the point. It never had been.

"We might not need the teaching," Lisa said. "But we like the company."

Carol's face changed. The guarded look fell away. "Is that so?"

"It is."

Dennis laughed. "You hear that, Carol? You're not getting rid of them that easy."

They waded back toward shore together, bags heavy, legs tired in that good way that came from an afternoon in the water. Lisa was thinking about what she'd said, how the words had come out without planning. She meant it. More than that, she'd come to count on it.

* * *

That evening, Nick fired up the grill while Lisa set the long table on the deck. She'd found a tablecloth somewhere, blue with white stripes, and weighted the corners with shells from the beach. Candles in mason jars. Mismatched plates she'd picked up at West End Garage.

"Fancy," Nick said, his eyes on the table.

"We're having people over. It should feel special."

Carol and Dennis arrived first, carrying a bowl of potato salad and a couple of baguettes. Roy came ten minutes later with a bag of corn so fresh the silk was still damp. Lisa and Nick had more clams than they could eat—the afternoon's haul piled in a bucket by the outdoor sink, already scrubbed and ready for the grill.

The space filled up. Nick manned the grill, working the clams open over the heat, brushing them with garlic butter. Dennis sliced the baguettes while Carol set out the potato salad. The corn went on last, the husks blackening over the flames while the kernels steamed inside.

Lisa stood at the edge of the deck, facing the bay. The water had gone pink and gold, the sky streaked with the last of the light. She could hear Carol laughing at something Dennis had said, Roy asking when the food would be ready, Nick calling out that the clams were done.

This deck had been Nick's when she moved in. His chairs, his grill, his view.

But tonight it was full of people she'd helped bring together. The table was set the way she liked it. The voices rising in laughter belonged to friends she'd made, not just inherited. When she turned around and saw Nick loading plates while Carol directed traffic and Roy actually smiled at one of Dennis's jokes, she realized the house didn't feel like his anymore.

It felt like theirs.

"Food's up," Nick announced.

They gathered around the table, passing plates and filling

glasses and talking over each other in that comfortable way that happened when people stopped being polite and started being themselves. Lisa sat between Carol and Nick, listening to stories about Dennis's years in the merchant marine, about Roy's decades as a commercial fisherman before his knees gave out.

The clams were perfect. The corn was sweet under its charred husk, the potato salad creamy and tangy. Lisa ate until she was full and then ate a little more because Roy had started making his own garlic butter and insisted everyone try his version.

Dennis stopped mid-sentence, squinting at the water. "What's that out there?"

Everyone looked. The bay had lost its color now, the last light fading behind the house, but something was moving out there. Shadows breaking the surface, catching the reflected glow from the deck lights.

Lisa stopped chewing.

The rays were back.

Dozens of them, maybe more, gliding through the shallows in that slow, undulating formation from the day she and Nick had nearly drowned. But they were farther out now, safely distant, their wings catching the light as they rose and fell.

"Cownose rays," Carol said. "The fever's still passing through. I've never seen them this close to shore after dark."

Everyone was standing now, moving to the deck rail to watch. Carol gasped as one of the larger rays lifted clear of the water, its wing tips in the air for a moment before it settled back down.

Nick's hand found the small of Lisa's back.

She looked at him. He was watching the rays, but he must have felt her gaze because he turned. They both remembered the panic—and the strange beauty of it.

The rays passed through in waves, their shapes growing smaller, less visible as they drifted away from shore. After a few minutes, the bay was calm again, just black water and the blinking of a channel marker in the distance.

"Well," Dennis said. "That's not something you see every day."

The gathering went on for another hour, the conversation easier now, punctuated by quiet stretches that felt natural rather than awkward. Around ten, Carol and Dennis said their goodnights. Roy left with them, offering nothing more than a raised hand and something that might have been "good clams."

When they were finally alone, Lisa and Nick sat on the deck together. The candles had burned down to stubs. Beyond the rail, the water lay flat and dark.

"This was a good night," Nick said.

"It was."

She rested her head against his shoulder. The deck creaked beneath their chairs, a familiar sound now.

"This feels different now," she said.

"What does?"

"All of it. The house. The deck. Being here." She watched the water, scanning for shapes that weren't there anymore. "I used to feel like I was visiting your life. Like I was staying in your guest room, even when I was sleeping in your bed."

Nick took his time answering. "And now?"

Lisa thought about the friends gathered around the table, the way she'd answered Carol's questions about Hawaii like she actually had stories worth telling. The rays had terrified her that first time. Tonight they'd been beautiful, watched from the safety of a deck she now thought of as her own.

"Now I'm not figuring out where I fit anymore," she said. "I'm already there."

The bay lay before them, dark and quiet. The clams in the sand, the rays passing through, the tides that would rise and fall tomorrow and the day after that.

She was home.

CHAPTER TEN

The Gyre was supposed to light up at 8:27, the exact minute the sun would drop below the tree line. Bo had calculated it himself using an app and what he called "forty years of paying attention to where things are in the sky."

Liz arrived at the Physick Estate grounds just after eight and found a gathering already forming. Word had spread about the collapse and the rebuild, and people wanted to see what had risen from the wreckage. She spotted familiar faces from the festival crew, a few volunteers she recognized from other installations, and a surprising number of locals who'd heard the story and come to witness the resurrection.

Greg was waiting for her near the rope line.

"Patrick's closing up the shop," he said. "I told him we had somewhere to be."

"You didn't have to come."

"Are you kidding? After everything you've told me about this thing? I'm not missing it."

She'd described the frantic hours of work, Bo and Paisley, the new design. Now, standing at the edge of the crowd with the rebuilt Gyre rising against the evening sky, she was glad he'd come.

The new structure was shorter than the original, maybe fourteen feet instead of twenty, but it spread wider, the spiral opening outward. Glass spheres clustered near the top—two dozen or so of the original sixty-three—and dozens of empty copper brackets dotted the structure where the rest should have been.

It was the empty mounts that elevated it. Deliberate. Intentional. Loss made visible. What survives, Liz had called it during the rebuild, and Bo had taken the concept and run with it.

"Wow," Greg said.

"Wait until it lights up."

Bo and Paisley were holding court near the base of the sculpture, surrounded by a small group of admirers. Paisley had added new flowers to her braid for the occasion, bright-orange marigolds mixed with the usual wildflowers, and she'd traded her paint-spotted smock for a flowing dress covered in a pattern that looked like exploding galaxies. Bo wore the same cargo shorts from the rebuild, but he'd put on a clean button-down, untucked, the sleeves rolled to his elbows.

"There she is!" Paisley spotted Liz and waved her over. "Our secret weapon. Come, come."

Liz made her way over, Greg following.

"This is Liz," Paisley announced to the group. "When our beautiful Gyre fell down and we were all standing around looking at rubble, she's the one who said, 'What if we make it mean something?'" She touched her heart with both hands. "What survives. Can you imagine? I've been doing this for thirty years, and I never would have thought of that."

"You would have eventually," Liz said.

"I would not have. I would have cried for three days and then gone back to Oregon." Paisley pulled Liz into a hug that smelled like sandalwood and patchouli. "You saved our art, and also possibly my week, because Bo does not handle disaster well."

"I handle disaster fine."

"He gets impossible. He once didn't speak for a week after a kinetic piece malfunctioned at a show in Portland."

"It attacked someone," Bo said.

"It grazed her. Three stitches." Paisley waved a hand. "The point is, Liz saved us from a week of Bo's silence, which, believe me, is not as peaceful as it sounds."

Greg leaned close to Liz's ear. "I like these two."

"Everyone does."

Bo had produced a tupperware container from one of his cargo pockets and was offering it to Greg. "Energy balls. Dates, almonds, coconut, and some lavender I picked from the estate garden."

"You picked their lavender?"

"It was overgrowing the path. I did them a favor."

Greg looked at Liz. She shrugged. He tried one, and his eyebrows went up. "That's good."

"He makes all his own food," Paisley said. "I haven't seen him eat anything pre-packaged in maybe fifteen years."

"Twelve," Bo corrected. "I bought crackers in 2013. There was an emergency."

"What kind of emergency requires crackers?"

"I don't want to talk about it."

The crowd had continued to grow. Liz estimated maybe eighty people now, spreading across the lawn, some sitting on blankets they'd brought, others standing in clusters, all of them watching the Gyre and the sky.

Megan appeared at Liz's elbow, slightly out of breath, her hair held up with what appeared to be a plastic fork from one of the food trucks. "I made it. Craig needed me to handle a thing with the sound system at the Light Forest, and then there was a parking situation on Washington Street, and I broke my last hair clip somewhere around hour fourteen of today." She touched the fork self-consciously. "This was the best I could do on short notice."

"It's working."

"It's really not, but I appreciate you saying that." She surveyed the crowd, the sculpture, the sky. "This is a good turnout. Better than I expected."

They stood together for a moment, watching the light fade.

"Listen," Megan said, her tone softening. "I know I've been a disaster. The whole festival, really." She shook her head. "Anyway, I just wanted to say thanks. For everything. For putting up with me. For being right when I was wrong about the duct tape thing."

"You weren't that wrong."

"I was completely wrong, and we both know it. But I appreciate you not rubbing it in." Megan straightened. "Also, I added you to my recommendation list. For future festivals. In case you ever want to do more of this."

Before Liz could respond, Bo's voice cut across the lawn.

"Three minutes!"

The crowd quieted, attention turning to the tower and the tree line where the sun was making its final descent.

Paisley had positioned herself near the control panel, a small box connected to the sculpture by cables that ran through the grass. Bo stood beside her, his phone out, watching the countdown on his app. The sky had turned purple and pink along the horizon, the first stars appearing overhead. The Gyre stood silhouetted against the fading light, its spiral form stark and strange, the empty mounts catching shadows.

"Thirty seconds!"

Everyone held their breath.

"Ten! Nine! Eight!"

People started counting along.

"Seven! Six! Five!"

"Four! Three! Two! One!"

Paisley pressed the button.

The Gyre came alive.

Light bloomed inside the glass spheres, soft at first, a pale gold that pulsed like a heartbeat. Then the color warmed, amber bleeding into orange, the spheres glowing like captured sunsets against the darkening sky. The light spread through the copper wire, tracing the spiral in threads of fire, illuminating the driftwood beams from within.

And then Liz saw what Bo had done with the empty mounts.

Each bracket held a small mirror, barely visible during the day, but now catching the light from the spheres and casting it outward in scattered beams. The effect was stunning. The missing spheres didn't leave darkness behind. They multiplied the light that remained, throwing it across the lawn in dancing patterns, touching the faces of the people watching, making the absence part of the beauty.

The crowd gasped. Someone started clapping, and then everyone was clapping, the applause sweeping toward them like a wave.

"Holy..." Greg didn't finish the sentence. He didn't need to.

Liz watched the light move through the sculpture, gold fading to rose, rose darkening to violet, the whole piece alive in a way that felt like watching time pass in fast motion. Sunset to twilight to starlight.

Bo and Paisley were hugging near the control panel. Megan had her phone out, filming. A child broke free from her parents and ran toward the rope line, the light painting her face in changing colors.

She thought of the Prism Corridor, the antechamber, how good it had felt to turn a problem into something better.

"I want to keep doing this," she said.

"The festival stuff?"

"Not exactly. I want to bring this feeling into Furnish and Feast. Events. Installations. Partnerships with local artists. Something that makes the shop more than just a shop."

Greg looked surprised, but not as much as she'd expected. "You've been thinking about this."

"I've been feeling it. I didn't have words for it until right now." She gestured at the sculpture, the lawn full of faces, the light still moving through the spiral. "This is what I want. Not at this scale. Something smaller. Something ours. But this feeling, creating something that brings people together. I need that to be part of what we do."

"Then let's figure out how to make it happen."

"You'd be okay with that? Hosting events, bringing in artists?"

"Liz." He stepped closer. "I'm in."

The sculpture cycled into a deep-blue phase, the spheres bright as stars, the mirrors scattering light across the lawn. People were taking photos, laughing, pointing out details to each other. A little boy sat cross-legged on the grass, his face tilted up, completely still.

Bo wandered over. "So? What do you think?"

"It's better than the original," Liz said. "By a lot."

"Paisley cried when we tested it last night. Actually cried. She said the mirrors were my best idea in twenty years." He looked back at it. "The mirrors only work because of the empty spaces. I never would have thought of that if the first one hadn't fallen."

"Sometimes you have to lose something to find out what it could become," Liz said.

* * *

Margaret had learned to recognize the particular energy of a shift's final hour. Visitors moved differently as the night deepened, their footsteps slower, their attention lingering. Children who'd been racing across the sand earlier now leaned against their parents, heavy-eyed but unwilling to leave. Couples stood at the water's edge, backlit by the glow of The Bloom, taking photos.

The days had started to blur together in the best way, one

evening flowing into the next, each shift bringing something new even as the rhythms stayed familiar.

Ruthie was back with the thermos. "Last one of the night."

Margaret accepted a cup and took a sip. Ruthie had gone with white wine sangria tonight—peaches and mint, something that tasted like summer itself.

"Craig said something interesting," Ruthie continued. "Apparently this is our last scheduled shift. Festival closes in two days, and they're consolidating the volunteer roster."

"Last shift?" Margaret looked out at the installation, the blue-green glow pulsing across the sand, visitors drifting through it. "I knew it was winding down, but I didn't realize we were finished."

"Neither did I until ten minutes ago." Ruthie settled into the beach chair beside her.

Dave and Hank were standing near the edge of the installation, talking to a family with two young boys who wanted to know how the lights worked. Margaret could hear Hank explaining about projectors and sensors with the same matter-of-fact authority he'd brought to identifying sand sharks and everything else the beach had thrown at them this summer.

"I'm going to miss this," Margaret said.

"The volunteering?"

"All of it. The evenings, having something Dave and I do together. Hanging out with you and Hank. Having a reason to sit on this beach for hours every night. The visitors, all of it." She watched a little girl run through the lit sand, her footsteps blooming bright behind her.

A commotion at the far end of the installation made them look up. Not the bad kind, not like the arguing couple from last week. This was laughter, excited voices, people pointing at something on the sand.

Margaret stood and walked toward the sound, Ruthie following. Near the dunes, a cluster of visitors had gathered around a section of the lit sand, all of them watching the ground.

Small shapes were darting across the surface, pale and quick, triggering the projections as they moved. Each time one crossed into range, the sand beneath it bloomed with color then faded as the shape raced on. There were dozens of them. Maybe more.

"Sandpipers," Dave said, appearing beside her. "A whole flock of them."

The birds were going berserk. Something about the lights, the motion-responsive technology, had caught their attention, and they couldn't stop investigating. They sprinted back and forth across the sand in tight zigzag patterns, their tiny legs a blur, each path leaving a trail of light behind them. When one bird triggered a flash, others would race toward it, which set off more flashes, which sent them scattering in new directions.

The installation had been designed for human visitors, for slow walks and contemplative pauses. The sandpipers had turned it into something else entirely, a frantic light show that painted the beach in swirling patterns no artist could have planned.

"Look at them go!" Ruthie had her phone up, recording. "They think they've discovered something."

"They have discovered something," Hank said. He'd joined them, his arms crossed, watching the chaos with an expression somewhere between amusement and grudging respect. "From their perspective, they just found a patch of sand that does magic."

More people wandered over, drawn by the noise. People who'd been heading toward the exit reversed course. Others pulled out phones to record.

Margaret found a spot beside Dave. The birds showed no sign of tiring. If anything, they seemed to be getting more enthusiastic, racing in patterns that grew increasingly elaborate, the lights strobing beneath them like a disco floor at a nightclub designed by seabirds.

Ruthie lowered her phone and caught Margaret's eye. "This is the best night of the whole run. I'm calling it now."

Eventually a dog barked somewhere down the beach and spooked them, the whole flock lifting off at once in a blur of wings and vanishing into the darkness over the dunes. The crowd applauded, actually applauded, as if they'd just witnessed the finale of a planned show.

The beach returned to its normal rhythms. Visitors spread out again. The four of them reclaimed their chairs near the volunteer station.

"The birds are always here this time of year," Hank said. "They just usually have better things to do than play with light art."

"Maybe they know it's almost over," Dave offered. "Getting their last show in before the festival closes."

The joke landed, but it lingered. Last show. Last shift. None of them said anything for a moment.

Around ten-thirty, a ghost crab scuttled out of the dunes and crossed into the installation, triggering a bloom of color before disappearing into the dark. Then another. For a few minutes, their pale shapes dotted the sand, setting off small flares of light as they hunted.

Ruthie poured the last of the sangria into four cups and handed them around.

"To the sandpipers," she said, raising hers.

"And the ghost crabs," Dave added.

"And the last shift," Hank said, though his voice had none of its usual gruffness.

Margaret raised her cup. "To whatever comes next."

They drank. The lights pulsed across the sand. Somewhere in the dunes, a sandpiper called once and fell silent.

CHAPTER ELEVEN

The evening sky was clear when Sarah pulled into Dorothy's driveway, the air still and heavy with June humidity. Dorothy was on the patio, arranging glasses, a pitcher of lemonade already sweating in the heat.

"Thirty-eight confirmed," Sarah said, setting down the box of books she'd carried from the car. "I capped the RSVPs yesterday. The mailing list has grown enough that I could have filled twice that."

"And the author?" Dorothy straightened a stack of napkins without looking up.

"Charlotte Tucker. She has a new essay collection out, got a nice review in The New Yorker, zero history of dramatic meltdowns or seagull impressions."

"You've thought of everything."

Sarah surveyed the garden. After the Norman Quick incident, she'd made a checklist. Every potential problem, every possible solution.

The roses were at peak bloom, the pathways freshly raked, the gazebo draped with string lights that would come on at dusk. Small lanterns lined the walkways, not yet lit. A folding table near the pergola waited for the potluck contributions guests would bring.

"It's beautiful," Sarah said.

Dorothy stood beside the koi pond, watching the fish move beneath the surface.

Sarah made two more trips to her car for the coolers of ice and the box of battery-powered candles she'd borrowed from the shop. The forecast had mentioned a chance of storms, but she wasn't worried. Locals called it the Cape May bubble—something about the bay and the ocean meeting that pushed most bad weather around the peninsula.

Guests began arriving around seven. Sarah recognized most of them—regulars from the Book Nook, familiar faces. Charlotte Tucker arrived at seven-fifteen, poised and professional in a simple navy dress, her reading materials already tabbed and annotated.

"What a stunning space," Charlotte said, helping herself to sparkling water from the refreshment table. "I've done readings in basements where the author outnumbered the audience. This is a significant upgrade."

Dorothy appeared beside them. "My husband designed it. Every path, every planting. He spent forty years getting it right."

"It shows." Charlotte's gaze traveled across the roses, the pergola, the gazebo where she would soon be reading. "There's intention everywhere. Nothing accidental."

Sarah watched them talk. Two women who'd never met, already comparing notes on roses.

The reading began at eight. Charlotte stood in the gazebo, the lights catching her silver earrings, and read from her latest collection.

Sarah sat near the back of the gathering and let herself enjoy the evening. The right author. The right crowd. The rules announced at the start, politely but firmly, and accepted without complaint.

She was thinking about the future, about what Books by Moonlight might become if they kept doing this, when she noticed the sky.

The western horizon had changed. Where clear blue had stretched toward sunset an hour ago, a bank of clouds now rose like a wall, dark and solid, the kind of formation that meant rain was minutes away, not hours. Sarah couldn't remember the last time she'd seen clouds build that fast.

Then the first gust of wind swept through the garden, bending the roses sideways and sending napkins scattering. Charlotte stopped mid-sentence, one hand going to her hair. "Well," she said into the rising wind, "that's one way to end on a cliffhanger."

"Ladies and gentlemen," Dorothy said, rising from her chair with the calm authority of someone who'd handled worse. "Let's move the reading inside, shall we?"

What followed was chaos. The wind picked up before anyone could organize, and then the rain came, not gradually but all at once, a sheet of water that turned the garden into a blur of motion and shouting voices. Sarah grabbed the box of books and ran for the house. Guests fled in all directions, some toward the house, others toward the gate, everyone suddenly soaked.

Sarah made it to the back porch and turned to look for Dorothy. The older woman was still in the garden, directing traffic, pointing people toward the kitchen door, utterly unconcerned about the rain plastering her silver hair to her forehead. A flash of lightning split the sky, and the thunder that followed rattled the windows.

"Dorothy! Come inside!"

Dorothy glanced at her, nodded once, and walked calmly through the downpour as if this were just another part of the evening's plan.

Inside, the house had filled with damp bodies and nervous laughter. Thirty or so people had crowded into Dorothy's ground floor, spreading through the sunroom, the living room, the kitchen. Water pooled on the hardwood floors. Someone was toweling off a woman who'd been caught near the koi pond.

Sarah stood in the hallway, her own shirt soaked through. The last Books by Moonlight at Dorothy's, washed out by a summer storm.

Dorothy was suddenly beside her, dripping but composed.

"This is interesting," she said.

"I'm so sorry. I should have watched the weather more closely."

"Sarah." Dorothy's voice was firm. "The weather is not your responsibility. The question is what we do now." She surveyed the group. "Everyone is here. Everyone is safe. We simply need to give them something to do."

She moved into the living room, and Sarah watched her work. A word here, a gesture there, groups forming and re-forming under her guidance. Within minutes, people had settled into corners and doorways, conversations starting up.

Someone found a deck of cards. A conversation started about everyone's worst weather stories. Laughter replaced the nervous energy.

Charlotte Tucker had been standing near the bookshelf, examining the spines. Now she turned to Dorothy, who was passing with a tray of rescued appetizers.

"Dorothy, I have an idea. Since Mother Nature clearly has opinions about my work, perhaps you might read something instead?"

Dorothy stopped. "I'm not an author."

"You don't have to be. This is your garden. Your home. Your story." Charlotte gestured toward the leather chair in the corner. "I noticed that chair when we came in. It looks well-loved."

"It was my husband's."

"Then perhaps there's something of his you could share. A

favorite poem, a passage he loved. Something that would honor what this evening was meant to be."

Sarah waited. The chair was Walter's spot. Dorothy hadn't moved anything since he died.

Dorothy stood very still. Outside, the storm continued to rage, rain lashing the windows, thunder rolling across the sky. Inside, the room had gone quiet.

"There's a book," Dorothy finally said. "Poetry. Walter read from it every evening, even near the end." She crossed to the chair and lifted a slim volume from the stack beside it. The cover was worn, the spine cracked from countless openings.

She sat down in Walter's chair.

People shifted to face her, finding spots on the floor and against the walls. Someone turned off the overhead light, leaving only the reading lamp and the spill of light from the kitchen doorway. The storm provided backdrop: wind and rain and the occasional flash of lightning through the curtained windows.

Dorothy opened the book to a marked page. Her hands were steady, her voice clear.

She read a poem about gardens—time passing, flowers blooming, a careful hand shaping the earth into something that would outlast the gardener. It was short, maybe twenty lines, and Dorothy read it simply.

When she finished, no one moved.

Then Dorothy turned to another marked page and read a second poem, this one about loss. Her voice caught once, near the middle, but she continued.

Dorothy closed the book and set it gently on her lap. She didn't look up right away. When she did, she was smiling.

"Walter would have enjoyed this," she said.

The applause started slowly and built until it filled the room. Dorothy accepted it with grace, nodding once, then standing and returning the book to its place beside the chair.

Charlotte finished her own reading while the storm wore

itself out. The living room crowd was more attentive than the garden audience had been—something about being stuck together, maybe.

The rain eased from deluge to drizzle around nine-thirty, the thunder moving east toward the bay. One by one, guests drifted toward the doors, testing the weather, finding it acceptable.

"We should check the garden," Sarah said.

They filed out through the back door, a smaller group now, maybe a dozen people who were curious enough to stay. The garden was transformed: paths turned to streams, flower beds flattened, lanterns knocked over and scattered. The chairs beneath the pergola had survived more or less intact, but the decorations were ruined, the lights in the gazebo hanging at odd angles.

The porch light caught the wet leaves, the roses drooping on their stems. The air smelled like earth and rain.

"Look at that," someone said.

They all turned toward the back fence, toward the climbing rose Dorothy had pointed out that first afternoon. The Desdemona. Walter's last.

The bud that had been waiting all week had opened. The bloom was enormous, white with the faintest blush of peach at its edges, its petals still wet from the rain.

Dorothy made a small sound, half gasp, half laugh. She walked slowly toward the rose, leaving the group behind, and stood before it with her hand pressed to her chest.

Sarah followed, stopping a few feet away, giving Dorothy space.

"He planted this two months before he died," Dorothy said quietly. "He said it reminded him of me. I never understood what he meant." She reached out and touched one of the petals, so gently that the water clinging to it didn't fall. "I think I understand now."

Behind them, guests were beginning to leave, voices calling goodbyes through the humid air.

Dorothy turned to Sarah. "All this chaos," she said, looking at the overturned lanterns. "Walter would have laughed."

* * *

Donna crested the dunes and stopped, her headlamp cutting a narrow path through the darkness ahead.

She'd been to Higbee Beach three or four times now, enough to recognize the best spots, to read the tide lines where fossils turned up. But at ten o'clock at night, with no moon and no other souls in sight, the familiar shoreline looked different.

"You coming?" she called back to Dale, who was still navigating the sandy trail behind her.

"Right behind you."

Clyde had mentioned night hunting days ago, during one of their early outings. The tides don't care what time it is, he'd said. And sometimes you find things at night that hide during the day. She was certain Garret had taken their bucket. Her mako tooth, gone. Donna had needed something to shake off that morning. A fresh start. A different kind of hunt.

Dale appeared beside her, his own headlamp bobbing as he adjusted the mesh bag clipped to his belt. They stood together at the top of the dune, looking out.

The beach had transformed. Without the sun to give it color and dimension, the sand stretched featureless in every direction, barely distinguishable from the water's edge. The moon hadn't risen yet, and the sky was thick with stars she'd never noticed before. The storm that had blown through earlier had scrubbed the air clean and maybe even churned up a few treasures. She could make out the Milky Way, an actual band of light overhead.

"Oh," Donna said, her voice barely above a whisper.

The sound of the water filled the darkness. During the day,

the waves were background noise. Now, in the stillness, the soft lap and pull of each one was all there was.

"It's like the bay got bigger," Donna said.

They made their way down to the waterline, lights sweeping the sand ahead of them. The tide was out, exposing a wide stretch of wet beach. Their beams picked up the dark bands of sediment and shell.

A shape moved at the edge of Donna's light.

She ducked instinctively as it swooped past her head, a dark blur cutting through her beam. Then another. And another.

"Bats," Dale said, tilting his light upward.

A dozen of them, maybe more, wheeling and diving over the beach. The lights had drawn clouds of moths and midges, and the bats had followed. Donna watched one pass so close she felt the air move against her cheek, then bank away into the dark.

"I've never seen them this close," she said.

"They're hunting the bugs around our lights." Dale tracked one with his beam as it spiraled upward. "We're basically a buffet."

"Come on," Donna finally said. "We didn't come out here to watch bats."

They found a promising stretch of shell and sand and set to work. The routine was familiar now: crouch, sift, examine, discard or keep. But at night, everything felt different. The lights created a narrow cone of visibility, forcing a tighter focus on each handful of sand.

The first hour passed quickly. Dale found three small teeth, nothing spectacular. Donna's bag held two teeth and something she thought might be a piece of whale bone.

The air carried the low-tide smell of exposed mud and salt, mixed with a greener note from the dune grass behind them. The bay water was warmer than the air, and when a wave washed over Donna's feet, the contrast made her shiver. Her knees were damp and gritty, her fingers pruny from sifting through handfuls of shell and sediment.

They worked in comfortable silence, ten feet apart, their beams occasionally crossing. Every few minutes, one of them would hold up a find for the other to see. Mostly it was nothing—a promising shape that turned out to be gravel, a fragment that was shell instead of tooth.

A fishing boat passed in the distance, its lights crawling across the dark water. Somewhere down the beach, an owl called twice and went silent.

"This is better than I expected," Dale said, not looking up from his patch of sand.

"The hunting?"

"All of it. The quiet. Being out here together." He sat back on his heels and stretched his neck, looking up at the stars. "We should do this more often."

Donna smiled to herself, knowing he couldn't see it. "Deal."

They kept at it. Dale found two more teeth, both larger than his earlier finds. Donna pulled something heavy from the wet sand and brushed it off.

"What've you got?"

She handed it to him. It was bone, dense and weathered, with a porous texture. About the size of his palm, curved slightly.

"I think it's part of a whale vertebra," Dale said.

Donna tucked it carefully into her bag. "I'm calling that a win regardless."

Around midnight, Donna's headlamp caught something in the sand that made her stop.

She'd been working a fresh patch exposed by the retreating tide, sifting mechanically. The beam passed over it, and she almost kept going. Almost dismissed it as another worn pebble or fragment of shell.

But she looked again.

The tooth was half-buried in the sand, only its edge visible.

Even in the artificial light, even with sand still clinging to its surface, Donna could see that it was different from anything she'd found before. Bigger. Much bigger. The dark enamel had a sheen to it.

She didn't reach for it right away. Part of her was afraid that if she touched it, it would turn out to be something else.

"Donna?" Dale's voice came from somewhere behind her. "You okay?"

She reached down and worked her fingers around the edges, loosening the sand's grip. The tooth came free with a wet sucking sound, and Donna held it up to the light.

Her hands were shaking.

The tooth was massive. At least four inches from root to tip, triangular, with fine serrations along both edges. The root was intact, fanning out at the base in a thick V-shape. Between the crown and the root, a darker chevron-shaped band marked what she recognized from her reading as the bourlette. The enamel was dark gray, almost black, and when Donna turned it in the light, she could see the mineral patterning that came from millions of years underground.

A megalodon tooth. Complete, undamaged, and bigger than any she'd ever seen outside of a museum display.

"Dale." Her voice came out strange, too high. "Come here. Now."

He appeared at her shoulder, his beam joining hers on the tooth. Neither of them spoke.

"That's not possible," Dale finally said.

"It's real. Feel it."

He took the tooth from her hands and turned it over, running his fingers along the serrations, testing its heft. His breath caught.

"Donna. Do you know what this is? Do you know how rare this is?"

"I know."

"This could be worth thousands of dollars." He looked at her then back at the tooth.

She nodded.

They stood there, passing the tooth back and forth, examining it from every angle.

Eventually, Donna wrapped the tooth in a bandana and placed it carefully in her bag. Her hands had stopped shaking.

"I think that's enough for tonight," he said.

They gathered their things and walked back toward the dunes, but neither of them was ready to leave. They found a spot above the high tide line and sat, side by side, facing the water.

"Fifteen years," Donna said.

"What?"

"Clyde said he's been hunting for fifteen years. Found two megalodons in all that time." She stretched her legs out in front of her. "I found one in a little over a week."

"Beginner's luck."

"I'll take it."

They sat for a while longer, listening to the bay.

Donna leaned against his shoulder. The megalodon tooth in her bag was perhaps fifteen million years old. And now she was the one holding it.

CHAPTER TWELVE

The last night of the Luminous Festival had brought half of Cape May out of their houses and into the streets. Judy could feel the energy as she and Bob walked toward Franklin Street, passing families heading to the beach installations, couples with cameras around their necks, children clutching glow sticks their parents had bought from the vendors.

Margaret, Dave, and the girls were already at Dylan's house with Fran, finishing up the tour of the tunnel and the speaking tube. Dylan had been happy to show anyone interested at this point—the more people who knew about the history beneath Franklin Street, the better. By the time Judy and Bob arrived, everyone was gathered on the porch.

"Perfect timing," Dylan said. "We're ready for the main event."

"Main event?" Bob asked.

Darren grinned. "Our neighbors have something to show you. Henry called us yesterday—said we needed to come see it."

* * *

The house next door to the Harrisons belonged to Marcy and Henry Rogers, who had lived there for twenty-five years. When they opened the door, Marcy couldn't stop smiling.

"We've walked past this place a thousand times," Dave said quietly as they filed inside. "Never knew anything was under it."

"Neither did we," Marcy said. "We thought the basement was just a basement."

Henry led them downstairs. The basement was neat and organized, shelves of storage boxes along one wall, a work-bench on another. Everyone looked toward the far corner.

A wooden door stood there, partially exposed. The paint around its edges had been scraped away, revealing dark wood beneath decades of accumulated layers.

"After we heard about the tunnels next door, I started poking around," Henry said. "I was already fixing some water damage, so I had the wall opened up. Started scraping and found this. At first I thought it was just old paneling. Then I found the hinges."

He'd cleared away enough paint to expose the door's outline, its handle, and part of its frame. The wood was oak, aged almost black, with hand-forged iron hardware that looked older than anything in the house above.

"We haven't opened it yet," Marcy said. "We wanted witnesses. And a historian." She nodded at Fran.

Fran approached the door slowly. She examined the frame, the hinges, the pattern of paint layers.

"This door is original to whenever the passage was built," she said. "Someone painted over it deliberately. Again and again, over decades. They were hiding it."

"Can we open it?" Margaret asked.

Henry produced a scraper and a small pry bar. "That's what we're here for."

The work took ten minutes. Judy watched as Henry freed

the door from the paint that had sealed it shut, Fran offering guidance when the old wood threatened to splinter. The rest of them stood back, flashlights ready.

Finally, Henry gripped the handle and pulled.

The door groaned open. Cool air rushed past them, carrying that same faint mineral smell. Flashlight beams criss-crossed as everyone aimed into the darkness beyond.

A passage. Narrower than Dylan's, with a lower ceiling. The walls were rough stone rather than brick, and the floor was hard-packed dirt, polished by years of use.

"How long do you think it's been sealed?" Dave asked.

"Decades, at least," Fran said. "Based on what we scraped off."

"Then we're the first," Bob said.

Fran ducked under the low lintel and went in. Judy followed close behind, then Bob, then the others in single file. The passage curved to the right within a few steps, blocking the light from the basement behind them.

Their flashlights revealed details as they moved forward. Wooden supports at irregular intervals, some showing signs of rot but most still solid. Scuff marks on the stone where shoulders had brushed against the walls over the years.

The passage widened into a room about ten feet square. Fran stopped short, and Judy nearly walked into her.

"Nobody touch anything," Fran said.

In the corner, a metal cot frame sat against the wall. A wool blanket, moth-eaten but recognizable, lay folded at one end. Beside it, a tin cup and a kerosene lantern rested on an over-turned crate. A pair of men's shoes, the leather cracked and curling, had been placed neatly beneath the cot.

"Someone lived here," Margaret said.

"Or hid here," Fran said. She swept her light across the room. "During Prohibition, if things got hot, you might need to disappear for a few days. What better place than a room nobody knew existed?"

Judy tried to imagine it—sleeping underground, no windows, no way to know if it was day or night above. Waiting for word that it was safe to come out.

Two passages led out of the room. Fran chose the larger one.

They walked for several minutes, the corridor turning sharply left, then right, then descending a set of rough-cut stairs. The walls changed from stone to brick and back to stone again. At one point they passed a bricked-up archway —another sealed connection to somewhere they'd never know.

"This wasn't all built at once," Fran said, running her hand along a seam where two types of stonework met. "Some of this is older. Coal cellars, maybe, or service access between properties. The bootleggers connected what was already here."

"We're under the street," Bob said. "We have to be."

No one argued.

The tunnel ended at a door—heavy timber with iron bands, never painted. It stood exactly as its builders had left it, the wood darkened with age.

Fran tried the handle. Stuck. She put her shoulder into it, but it didn't budge.

"Locked from the other side," she said.

Silence. And then Judy heard it—faint, muffled, but clear. Music. Voices. The clink of glasses.

"There's people on the other side," Bob said.

Fran knocked. Nothing. She knocked harder.

"They can't hear you over the noise," Dave said.

"Everyone," Fran said. "Together."

They lined up and pounded on the door, all of them at once. Bob shouted "Hello!" and the others joined in—Henry loudest of all, which no one expected.

The music stopped.

Footsteps approached. A lock turned—then another. The door swung inward, and a man's face appeared in the gap—

beard, bar towel over his shoulder. His expression went from confused to alarmed to amazed.

"What the—?" he said.

"Hi," Fran said. "We came from Franklin Street."

He stepped back, and Fran climbed past him, then Judy, then the rest of them, one by one, blinking as they emerged into the back of a bar.

A dozen customers stared at them. Someone's drink was frozen halfway to their mouth.

"Did you just come out of the basement?" a woman at the bar asked.

"There's a tunnel," Henry said, as if that explained everything.

The bartender looked at the group—dusty, kids and grandparents and everyone in between—and started laughing.

"I've worked here three years," he said. "Owner told me that door's been locked since before he bought the place. Said it probably led to an old coal cellar." He looked past them into the darkness. "Guess not."

Fran was already pulling out her phone. "What's the address here? I need to document this."

"You're at the Crabby Anchor," he said. "Washington Street."

"This building's old enough," Fran said, glancing at the tin ceiling and the original woodwork behind the bar. "Wouldn't surprise me if this was a speakeasy back in the day. That tunnel wasn't just for escape—it was for delivery."

"We walked from Franklin," Bob said. "Underground."

The bartender shook his head, still grinning. "First round's on me. Anyone who comes out of my basement wall deserves a drink."

They didn't stay long—just long enough to catch their breath, answer a few questions from curious patrons, and watch Fran photograph the door from this side. Then they said their goodbyes and walked out the front entrance onto Washington Street, emerging into the festival crowd like they'd just stepped out for air.

"That was not how I expected tonight to go," Margaret said.

"Twenty-five years we've had that door in our basement," Henry said. "Never knew where it led."

"We should get back," Marcy said. "Lock up the door to the tunnel."

They headed off toward Franklin Street while the rest of them lingered on Washington Street. The festival was still going strong around them.

"I need to get the Historical Society involved," Fran said. "First thing tomorrow. That tunnel, the hiding room, all of it. This is significant."

Fran waved and walked to her car, already typing notes into her phone.

That left Judy and Bob, Margaret and Dave, and the girls. They glanced at each other, a little dazed.

"So," Margaret said. "Beach?"

They made their way through the historic district, taking their time. Smaller installations had been scattered throughout the neighborhood—a projection of wildflowers blooming across a clapboard house, a fence woven with fiber optic threads pulsing like a constellation, a sound installation hidden in a garden that layered ocean waves with wind and birdsong.

The streets led them toward the beach. As they approached the promenade, Margaret spotted familiar faces in the crowd. Sarah and Chris near the coffee vendor. Donna and Dale studying one of the light sculptures. Lisa and Nick on a bench by Congress Hall. Liz walking with Greg, both of them looking tired but satisfied.

Everyone had come out for the final night.

Victorian houses gave way to sand. The beach installations glowed against the night sky.

The ocean stretched beyond them, the same water that had

carried ships and smugglers and secrets for centuries. The lighthouse flashed in the distance, steady and patient. Just another night in Cape May—and all the mysteries still waiting to be found.

EPILOGUE

A week after the festival ended, Cape May had quieted down.

Margaret was in the garden, pulling weeds between the tomato plants, when Dave came out the back door with the mail.

"Anything good?" she asked, not looking up.

"Bill, bill, junk, and..." He held one up. "Something for you. Handwritten."

That got her attention. She stopped mid-pull and tugged off her gardening gloves. Dave handed her a cream-colored envelope with her name and address written in dark-green ink. The penmanship was elegant, old-fashioned. There was no return address.

She opened it carefully. Inside was a single card:

Dear Margaret,

You are cordially invited to join the Opalescent Society. We are a small group devoted to the cultivation of beauty, the preservation of tradition, the romanticizing of everyday life, and the quiet joys of noticing things.

Our next gathering will be held on the first Saturday of July at a location to be disclosed upon your acceptance.

We hope you will consider becoming one of us.

No names. No phone number. Just a small embossed periwinkle bow at the bottom.

"Opalescent Society?" Dave read over her shoulder. "I've never heard of them."

"Neither have I." Margaret turned the card over. Nothing on the back.

"You going to accept?"

"I don't even know how."

Dave shrugged. "Cape May. Probably someone will just show up and ask."

Margaret ran her thumb over the periwinkle bow.

"You're curious," Dave said.

"I am."

He smiled. "Good. I'd be worried if you weren't."

Margaret slipped the card back into its envelope and tucked it into her apron pocket. For now, the weeds weren't going to pull themselves.

But as she turned back to the tomatoes, she was already wondering about the kind of people who formed societies devoted to the quiet joys of noticing things.

Whatever the Opalescent Society was, she intended to find out.

* * *

Pick up book 20 in the Cape May Series, **Cape May Whimsy,** to follow Margaret, Liz, Dave, and the rest of the bunch. Preorder coming soon!

Start book 1 in my new Ocean City series, **A Summer in Ocean City.**

. . .

Begin the **Sea Isle City** series with **The Sea Isle Summer Rental**.

ABOUT THE AUTHOR

Claudia Vance is a writer of Women's Fiction and Clean Romance. She writes feel good reads that take you to places you'd like visit with characters you'd want to get to know.

She lives with her boyfriend and 2 cats in a charming small town in New Jersey, not too far from the beautiful beach town of Cape May. She worked on television shows and film sets for many years. She's an avid gardener and nature lover.

www.ingramcontent.com/pod-product-compliance
Lightning Source LLC
Chambersburg PA
CBHW030933060726
47591CB00005B/1784